FAKE IT TILL
YOU MAKE IT

Praise for M. Ullrich

Life in Death

"Such a joy to discover a 'different' romance with more mature women going through a real life scenario and an author who gets her teeth into gritty and difficult subjects with style and grace. Absolutely excellent reading."
—*Lesbian Reading Room*

"The pain at times is palpable, tears streaming down your face as you feverishly read, totally engrossed in the story. Is it good? Oh my goodness yes, this book is very good."
—*The Romantic Reader Blog*

Fortunate Sum

"Sometimes there is nothing that can entertain you or make you feel better than a well written and thoroughly captivating romance. This book does this and more. A love story that is as delightful as it is engaging."—*Inked Rainbow Reviews*

By the Author

Fortunate Sum

Life in Death

Fake It till You Make It

Visit us at www.boldstrokesbooks.com

FAKE IT TILL YOU MAKE IT

by

M. Ullrich

2017

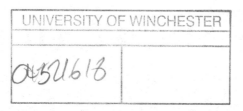

FAKE IT TILL YOU MAKE IT

ISBN 13: 978-1-62639-923-5

This Trade Paperback Original Is Published By
Bold Strokes Books, Inc.
P.O. Box 249
Valley Falls, NY 12185

First Edition: June 2017

CREDITS
EDITOR: JERRY L. WHEELER
PRODUCTION DESIGN: STACIA SEAMAN
COVER DESIGN BY JEANINE HENNING

Acknowledgments

I'm still in shock that this is my third novel. I thought the third time would be the charm with acknowledgments, but I was wrong. I still don't know how to put my gratitude into words.

First, I must thank everyone at Bold Strokes Books. I'm surrounded by boundlessly talented and incredibly supportive people. I'm honored to be a part of this family. Sandy and Radclyffe took one heck of a chance on me, and I'm determined to make the most of the opportunity I've been given.

My editor, Jerry Wheeler, has done the impossible yet again. You're a wonderful teacher, Jerry, and a patient, talented man. Thank you for seeing my vision and explaining how I can make it into the best version of itself. I become a more confident writer with each book because of you, and for that I'll always be grateful.

Monika, you sweet and accident-prone woman, thank you for your friendship and for never hesitating to share your most embarrassing moments with me. This book wouldn't be half as entertaining if I didn't have such unbelievable true events to build a love story around.

To write about love is to know love, and, Heather, you make it easy for me to imagine a hundred ways for my imaginary people to fall in love. Thank you for your excitement, your support, and your patience. I'm not easy to deal with when I'm facing a deadline or when my focus is in fiction as opposed to our reality. I love you endlessly, and please keep kicking me in the butt when I slack off. Kthanksbye.

Kris and Maggie: #TOTU game on.

I'd love to thank each and every reader individually, but since that's not possible, this is my thank you to you all. Whether you've been on board with me since book one or this is the first book of mine you've chosen to read, thank you so very much.

I hope the humor in this book is able to brighten, if only for a moment, some of the darkness we're seeing in the world today. Peace and love, always.

To Heather,
For standing beside me as we take on life one step at a time.

Step One

Getting Started

This latest job listing had it all: a guarantee of health benefits, sick time, and paid vacation, but most importantly the promise of a fresh start far away from Genevieve Applegate's hometown of Milan, Pennsylvania. Genevieve wasn't blind to the small town's charms, but even the most charming of towns grows old after living there every day. Twenty-seven years was a long time for someone who dreamed of more money, more growth, and more of a life.

She had a set Friday night routine. After a particularly long week working for the local newspaper, Genevieve would settle down in front of her personal computer with her favorite beer and pull up a plethora of updated job listings. Job hunting was both comforting and invigorating. Each listing she qualified for brought forth new daydreams and possibilities, but she hadn't applied to any until now.

Boasting terms such as "up and coming" and "forward thinking," the posting lit her blue eyes. The magazine was also one of the top-selling publications at the Jersey Shore. Genevieve smiled to herself as the image of grassy dunes and multicolored sunrises across the Atlantic came to mind. It seemed perfect, the glass slipper she had been waiting for. She read every other word before moving the cursor to the bottom of the page, hovering above the bright blue button that'd lead her to the application page. The catchy tune of her ringing cell phone distracted her. A meek smile spread across her pink lips as she took in the name that lit up the display.

"Hello, Jeremy," Genevieve said coyly and tucked a strand of her strawberry-blond hair behind her ear.

"Hey, babe, are you home?"

"Yeah, I got home a little while ago." She took a quick look at the clock in the corner of her monitor. She had already been home for three hours. *Time flies when you're looking for a new life,* she thought.

"Would you like some company? I've finished up my grading and lesson plans for next week. The weekend is all ours." Genevieve could hear the suggestive smile in Jeremy's voice, but she kept her eyes on her computer screen.

"For a gym teacher you sure do have a lot of paperwork."

"Gym teachers are still teachers, you know. Plus, they have me teaching three health classes this quarter. It's killing me."

"Less basketball and more puberty talk. Sounds horrid."

"Don't forget safe sex and pregnancy."

"My favorite memories of high school." Genevieve laughed lightly, and her smile broadened when Jeremy joined in. "I'm sorry to disappoint, but I'm busy tonight."

"Going out or staying in?"

"Staying in." She looked at the listing again and took her thumbnail between her teeth. She was hesitant to share her excitement prematurely, but the need to talk about this new possibility was too strong. "I may have found my dream job."

"Oh? Has the search finally come to an end?" She could hear the eye roll in his voice. Jeremy hinted at the years she had spent looking for that diamond in the rough, the one job that would finally open a door larger than that of an outhouse. "Tell me about it."

"There's not much to tell right now. I don't want to speak too soon, but it has every keyword I've been looking for, and it's in New Jersey."

"Are you for real, Gen?"

"I'm tired of doing and seeing the same things every day, Jeremy. I'm not like you. I don't find comfort in routine, I find it stifling."

"I know."

"If I have to do another year at *The Morning Sunrise*, I'm going to go crazy. I can only write so many engagement announcements and county fair reviews before I go mad." Genevieve clicked on the apply button, and her heart skipped slightly when the next page loaded. "The most creative column I wrote this year was about a snowdrift shaped like a sailboat. Riveting." She took a sip of her Budweiser that had been sitting beside her computer. Her friends never understood how she could drink room-temperature beer, but Genevieve found a Bud dependable in its delicious satisfaction.

"But that last fair made for such a great article," Jeremy said. He chuckled deeply into the phone.

"A kettle corn stand going up in flames made the cover, yeah, but I want to write articles that help people." *I want to meet new people, too,* Genevieve thought. Growing up in a small town limited her interactions. She knew everyone's story because they either grew up with her or helped raise her. Inspiration was hard to find. "I proposed a cultural piece today, and I got laughed at. *Laughed at,* Jeremy. I would've been humiliated if I didn't already know far more embarrassing things about my coworkers."

"What makes you so sure that this new job will give you everything you're looking for?"

"I'm not certain." Genevieve started to fill in her information in the blank boxes. "But it's the most promising listing I've seen in a while."

"I know you're going to do whatever you want to do in the end, but will you at least think about it a little longer? Maybe through the weekend? We both know how you have a tendency to act a bit *too* spontaneously sometimes. You walk into a new situation with blinders on half the time."

"I don't," Genevieve said. She bit the inside of her cheek to keep from lashing out at Jeremy. He was just being the cautious, logical boyfriend he had been since they had started dating their senior year of high school. Jeremy had even been hesitantly understanding of Genevieve's refusal to entertain the idea of marriage until her career path was in place. She knew this job could mean the first significant change in their relationship, so she couldn't blame him for wanting her to take her time with a decision. "I'll think about it."

"Good."

"I'm surprised you're not pushing me to apply."

"Why is that?"

"Because the sooner I land my dream job, the sooner you land your dream wife."

"This is true. I should be applying *for* you." He laughed lightly, and Genevieve finished her beer before Jeremy changed the subject. "Are we still on for tomorrow night? Ben and Theresa are expecting us."

"We'll be there." Two of Genevieve's friends from grade school had gotten engaged a month earlier. She was honored to write up the announcement for them. "You know how much I *love* engagement parties."

"You're being sarcastic."

"Am I?" She rolled her neck and sighed when she felt a satisfying pop.

"This one will be fun. They're having it in the Andersons' barn."

"I had my first kiss in that barn, and I saw a horse euthanized there as well." The memory caused Genevieve to shudder.

"There'll be no horses, but Tommy Fowler will be there. Maybe he'll be looking for a reenactment."

"Too bad he's married."

Jeremy laughed. "I'll pick you up tomorrow at six. I love you, Gen."

"Love you, too." Genevieve ended the call and turned her attention back to her empty beer bottle. Another Budweiser would do her good. She went to the kitchen, a short distance from the small corner of the living room she called her office. When she came back with a fresh beer, she stood in the middle of her small, one-bedroom house and thought of what to do next.

Genevieve was already in a T-shirt and sweatpants by nine o'clock. She took a sip of her cold beer before looking between her worn, inviting couch and her computer. The screen was still alive and bright, yet to be put to sleep by the timed screensaver. She had recorded several shows and had even more books piled up that she had been meaning to read. Genevieve was about to retreat to her king-sized bed and lose herself to fictional characters for hours when a late summer breeze came through an open window causing the houseplant on her desk to sway invitingly, beckoning her back to the computer like come-hither fingers.

"I thought about it long enough," Genevieve muttered to herself and marched back to her computer. She uploaded her tweaked resume and proofread every piece of information she had offered up. She was an experienced writer looking for the challenge of a new job in a new environment. Genevieve took another quick glance at the company's title. She was strongly tempted to click on the link and peruse the website, but Genevieve was a firm believer in fate, jinxing the good, planets aligning, and letting destiny do its thing. She submitted her application with one comforting truth echoing in her mind: *Out Shore Magazine* would be lucky to have her.

STEP TWO

Be Careful with Your Introductions

Genevieve's predictable life allowed her to do just that—predict. She could predict the exact time her neighbor would start to mow his lawn on a Saturday morning, when the local market stocked the freshest produce, and whose birthday would be celebrated that week in the neighborhood.

What Genevieve didn't predict was a phone call first thing Monday morning from Dana at *Out Shore Magazine* asking if she'd be available the next day for an interview. Every moment from then to her arrival in Asbury Park, New Jersey, was a blur. Genevieve stared into the mirror and looked over her simple black pantsuit with a scrutinizing eye. She had been blessed with genes that allowed her face to appear ageless, fresh and far younger than her twenty-seven years, but sometimes she felt it was more of a curse. She looked like an adolescent dressed in her mother's clothes.

"Lose the jacket," she said to her reflection. She tossed the black blazer onto the bathroom countertop. Genevieve unbuttoned the first two buttons on her green shirt, opening the collar just enough to ease her breathing. "Calm down," she prepped herself, "talk about your work and you'll be fine." She ran her damp palms along her tight ponytail. "Too severe." Genevieve checked her watch and removed the small elastic from her hair. She ran her shaky fingers through the straightened strands and reevaluated her image. "Better." She turned abruptly and made her way back to the reception area. Before Genevieve could take a seat, a casually dressed young woman approached her.

"Ms. Applegate?"

"Yes," Genevieve said while straightening her posture subconsciously.

"I'm Dana Matheson, Harper Davies's assistant." Dana extended her hand quickly, and Genevieve fumbled with her portfolio folder.

"Nice to meet you."

"Ms. Davies is ready when you are." Dana started to lead the way through a labyrinth of desks and work stations.

The office was wide open, outlined by an abundance of tall windows that lit the space with a natural, therapeutic glow. Genevieve knew how much of an improvement it'd be from the harsh yellowed lighting at the *Sunrise*.

"Have a seat." Dana gestured to one of two soft leather chairs just inside the office. "Can I get you anything? Water, coffee…"

Genevieve declined the offer politely, and Dana left. Once she was alone, Genevieve glanced around the small office. The desk was tidy, and framed covers of past issues lined the walls. Before she could get a close look, however, she sensed someone beside her.

"Sorry to keep you waiting." Genevieve turned in her seat, the leather protesting loudly against the material of her pants. "Ms. Applegate," said a tall woman her right hand outstretched, "I'm Harper Davies."

"I…it's…" Genevieve tripped over the greeting she'd rehearsed when she met Harper Davies's gaze. She took a breath to steady herself. "It's nice to meet you, Ms. Davies."

"Harper, please." She smiled broadly, showing deep dimples on either side of brilliant white teeth. "Only Dana calls me Ms. Davies, and that's because she refuses to listen to me." Harper chuckled.

"Then I think I should tell you no one calls me Ms. Applegate." Genevieve relaxed her shoulders and crossed one leg over the other. "Genevieve will work, but most people call me Gen." Harper turned her lips up slightly, the motion barely qualifying as a smile, but Genevieve was struck by how her whole face softened.

Harper finally took her seat behind the desk. Genevieve watched as she moved, noting the woman's tall, slender build. The cut of her charcoal suit accentuated her broad shoulders, and the cobalt shirt she wore did wonders for her already captivating gray eyes. Genevieve looked away abruptly so she wasn't caught staring. She looked at her own reflection in a decorative mirror set off to the side of the room. Her cheeks were rosy with a natural blush, and the dark rings of perspiration around the armpits of her shirt showed the pressure of the moment. Genevieve's right hand flew to the crease of her left arm to assess the damage and cover it up. She cursed her choice of silk blends and a color that changed when dampened.

"Genevieve?"

"Hmm?" She looked back to Harper with wide eyes and embarrassment coloring her face. She could have fixed this by putting her jacket on, if only she hadn't left it in the bathroom. "Damn it," Genevieve said under her breath.

"I'm sorry?" Harper looked on with obvious concern.

"Nothing, I'm sorry." Genevieve clamped her arms tightly against her torso and tried her best to feign a relaxed demeanor. "It's warmer than I expected it to be today."

"It's the windows." Harper turned in her chair and

motioned to the large panes of perfectly clear glass. "They let in so much sun on days like this, it tends to feel like we're kept in a warming box. I can get you a bottle of cold water." Harper started to stand.

"No, I'm fine." Genevieve waved off her concern and offer, but tried to keep her arms down. "Thank you."

"If you say so." Harper sat back and looked at Genevieve silently for a moment before speaking. "I looked over your resume. You've been working at," She looked at the paper in front of her briefly, "*The Morning Sunrise* for over five years now. You must've become quite the asset there."

"I wouldn't say that." Genevieve reminded herself she had to balance confidence and modesty. "But they knew they could rely on me and my flexibility."

"What made you look elsewhere?"

Genevieve shrugged. "I grew tired of the same old, same old. I'm ready to spread my wings and see exactly where my aforementioned flexibility could take me."

Harper picked up a pen and tapped it against the hard surface of the desk. "What did you do before this job?"

"I worked for my school paper and did some freelance writing. You'll see on my resume that I'm very active with several different blogs of varying subject matter across the web."

"I noticed." Harper dropped her pen and crossed her arms over her chest. When the silence stretched on, Genevieve's nerves grew shaky. They looked at one another, and Genevieve felt distinctly like she was being evaluated.

"Ms. Davies, I—"

"We agreed on Harper, Genevieve." Genevieve muttered an apology and Harper continued smoothly, "I have to be honest with you." Genevieve's spirits started to sink. "Your resume, though impressive in its own right, doesn't necessarily scream *Out Shore* material."

"Then why did you call me in?" She tried to keep the tightness from her voice, but she still sounded curt.

"Because that made you stand out from the other applicants. I'm constantly being told what other publications did and how other journalists and writers wrote about A, B, and C to help their employers succeed, but never once have I met an applicant so straightforward about wanting this job for their own personal gain. Your cover letter was about what a position here would mean for your own career growth. You believe *Out Shore* would do that for you?"

"Absolutely," Genevieve said without hesitation.

"*Out Shore Magazine* is everything to me, and my goal is for it to become the premier LGBT publication on the East Coast, if not nationwide. I want to rival *The Advocate* and leave just as great a legacy behind." Harper leveled Genevieve with a steely gaze that hinted at the seriousness of her plans. "It seems that you already know what we have to offer, so what can you bring to the table that'll help make that happen?"

Genevieve's head was spinning but her vision was becoming clearer than ever. Her surroundings came into focus, minute details of rainbow flags and Pride Parade centerfolds now front and center in those framed covers. Harper's short cropped and perfectly styled hair, menswear fashion, and makeup-free face also made more sense. *Androgynous,* she thought. She'd read the word somewhere before and was finally able to put it in place. She kicked herself. But Harper was expecting an answer.

"What I can offer is…" Genevieve looked beyond Harper, out to the sprawling landscape outside the large window. An eclectic city just waited to be discovered, and the promise of sandy beaches sat upon the horizon. She needed to make this move. *Confidence and modesty,* she reminded herself.

"As a young lesbian from a small, conservative community, I believe I can offer readers a fresh perspective on daily life. This certainly isn't Milan, Pennsylvania, anymore, and I do believe a lot of women and men can identify with this type of significant life change." She spoke seamlessly, and when the words stopped flowing, Genevieve took a deep breath, hoping to steady the dizzy life changes scrambling her unsteady mind.

Harper's reaction was unreadable at first. The corner of her mouth twitched, hinting at a smirk. Genevieve waited patiently for the woman across from her to seal her fate, one way or another.

"Well, Genevieve, when can you start?"

Genevieve smiled brightly. "Right away!" Her enthusiasm must've been contagious because Harper's grin matched her own. *I did it!* Genevieve thought as she stood unsteadily once she reached her full height. Harper escorted Genevieve back into the open office and she took stock again of her new workplace and each smiling face that greeted her politely. *I really did it.*

STEP THREE

Don't Offer Up Too Much Information

I wish you would tell me more about this new job."

"You know how I feel about jinxing things, Jeremy," Genevieve said as she directed him up the stairs. "I feel good about it. Really good."

"I bet you told Chloe all about it," Jeremy said. His jealousy toward Chloe never ceased to amaze Genevieve. Yes, she had a tendency to share every detail of her life with her best friend first, but not even Chloe was privy to this.

"It's a cultural magazine that's really making its mark amongst similar publications. That's all I told Chloe, and that's all I'm telling you." Genevieve shoved Jeremy playfully, and he fumbled the box in his hands as he set it down.

"Fine," he said, raising his hands in surrender. "I think that's the last one."

"Fifty small boxes. I could've done it in six large ones." Genevieve surveyed the sea of brown cubes that filled her new small, one-bedroom apartment. She put her hands on her hips. "My mother insisted there's a special packing technique I'm unaware of."

"Maybe there is." Jeremy turned to Genevieve. He wrapped his arms around Genevieve's slim waist and pulled her close. "Or maybe she just wanted you to take your time packing so you'd stick around longer."

Genevieve sank into Jeremy's embrace easily. He was a husky man and stood at just over six foot three, which was a substantial difference from her petite, five-foot-two build. She felt safe with him. Comfortable. "That's a devious plan."

"We're all going to miss you."

"I'm five hours away," Genevieve said as she pushed back from him. "It's not cross-country."

Jeremy looked at his watch and kissed the top of Genevieve's head. "That's five hours I better start tackling now. I'm sorry I can't spend the night with you." Jeremy looked genuinely distraught.

"It's okay," Genevieve reassured him, fighting the relief and happiness she felt at having her first night to herself from appearing on her face. She hugged her boyfriend one last time before leading him to the door, where she stood on her toes to kiss him good-bye. She squealed in surprise when he lifted her off her feet and pressed her against the hardwood of her door. He kissed her deeply, and when he pulled back, a bright smile lit his boyish face.

"I'm really going to miss you, Gen." He kissed her again and set her back on her feet. "I love you."

"Love you, too." She watched as he trotted to his truck.

Genevieve shut the door quietly. Her slight smile faded as she thought about her preparations for the next day. In less than twenty-four hours, she would be a different Genevieve.

❖

8:49 am. Genevieve looked at the face of her watch for the third time in less than two minutes and back to the glass double doors before her. She believed arriving ten minutes early was an easy display of professionalism and made a great first impression.

Genevieve started a mental checklist, reviewing the little details about her backstory in preparation for making small talk as a newbie. *Never use pronouns when talking about relationships. Everything else can remain the same.* She inhaled the clean September air deeply. *Just don't forget that you're a lesbian now.* She fidgeted with a thin silver ring on her middle finger, spinning it around and around as she controlled her breathing.

"Are you going to stand there all day? Some of us have a job to get to." Genevieve started at the sudden voice that barked from behind her. She turned and came face-to-face with a stunning redhead, though the woman's natural beauty did little to soften her snarl.

"I'm sorry." Genevieve moved to the side and let the woman pass. Her apology went unacknowledged. When she looked at her watch again, she realized she'd only be five minutes early. "Damn." She didn't get more than fifty feet into the office before Dana greeted her.

"Good morning, Ms. Applegate."

Genevieve smiled politely and adjusted the purse she had slung on her left shoulder. "Call me Gen, please."

"Good morning, Gen." Dana didn't miss a beat. "Welcome to *Out Shore Magazine.* I'll take you on a quick tour of the office, making sure you know where all the important things are." Genevieve found keeping up with the young assistant hard as she weaved around rows of desks. "Like the break room and bathrooms." Dana pointed off to the left where a modest-sized room held a refrigerator, tables, and two coffee machines. Genevieve stared on with happy relief.

Better than the instant they supplied us with at my last job.

"Gen?" Dana looked at her expectantly before continuing the tour. "This way please."

Genevieve continued to follow and tried her best to not shrink under every curious and calculating gaze that followed her. She'd forgotten what it was like to be the new kid in town. Actually, she'd never really known that feeling. Even at her last job she had worked with friends she grew up with or their parents. Upon this realization, Genevieve's palms grew sweaty and her breathing shortened as if she had run her way through the office. She was new, *this* was all new. No familiar faces or friends to fall back on. Just strangers. *What have I gotten myself into?*

"This is your desk." Dana pointed proudly toward a clean, organized workspace flanked by two occupied desks. "Maxine and Matthew will be your neighbors." A middle-aged butch woman looked up at Genevieve and offered her a kind smile. Maxine's dark eyes held a hint of unwavering youth, but her spiked salt-and-pepper hair and laugh lines gave her true age away. She offered Genevieve her left hand.

"Nice to meet you…?"

"Maxine, Matthew—this is Genevieve Applegate."

"Call me Gen."

Matthew shot Genevieve a blinding smile. "Another woman? I thought I told Harper to hire a hunk this time around." He had naturally platinum hair, impeccably sharp style, blue eyes, and charm for days. "Where do I go to complain?" He shook Genevieve's hand and followed it up with a wink.

"I'll make sure to put out a suggestion box just for you, Matthew," Dana joked. She turned her attention back to Genevieve just as she settled in at her desk. "Ms. Davies is out of the office today, but she wanted me to give you your first assignment." Genevieve swallowed hard. "She wants you to write," Dana said simply.

Befuddled, Genevieve raised a skeptical eyebrow. "What?"

"She wants you to write," Dana repeated.

"Yes, I understand that, but write *what*?" Genevieve looked back and forth between Matthew and Maxine, who were both grinning widely, their amusement thinly veiled. "What am I missing?"

"Everyone spends their first day writing everything and anything that comes to mind," Maxine said.

"Ms. Davies likes to have a sampling of your style as well as preference of topics. Think variety and quality. Turn in as many pieces as you can by five o'clock," Dana said, turning away before Genevieve could ask for more direction.

"I can't decide if I'm intimidated or inspired by her." Genevieve wondered the words aloud.

"A balance of both, I assure you," Maxine said.

"And you'll probably have a crush on her by the end of the week." A sultry, oddly familiar voice spoke up from behind Genevieve's chair.

"Clarissa, meet Gen—the new hire," Matthew said.

"The roadblock is the new hire?" She was immediately speared by Clarissa's predatory green eyes and flustered by her menacing smile. Clarissa swept a lock of auburn hair over her shoulder. She propped one hand on her cocked hip, still toying with the ends of her hair. "I should've known. You were obviously frozen in fear earlier. Let me guess…first job?"

"No—"

"I'm surprised. I'll see you later for lunch, Matthew. I want to hear all about your date last night." Clarissa was gone as quickly as she had come, leaving Genevieve shaken and annoyed.

"Don't let her get to you," Maxine said. "She's not all bad, she just makes it her mission to traumatize and embarrass new hires, especially the young and pretty ones. You'll get used to it. Before you know it, she'll target someone else."

"*Great.*" Genevieve looked at the clock. It was just after nine, and she felt as if she had lived an entire day already. Meeting new coworkers was exhausting, especially when you were there under false pretenses. She closed her eyes and took a deep, cleansing breath, listening to the noise of many keyboards around her telling stories and producing news for the masses. Genevieve was in her element. She was made for journalism, and she wouldn't let one little detail derail just how good this opportunity could be for her, or how much her column could mean for readers.

She stretched her palms out against the surface of her desk and let the coolness of the surface penetrate her skin. After balling her hands into fists and releasing them several times, Genevieve opened a new Word document and started to type. First, she wrote an article about weather predictions for the upcoming winter and deleted it immediately. Next, she did a nonfictional story about a breakup she had experienced secondhand through Chloe, but she erased that document shortly after lunch, once she realized making her mark as a relationship columnist would be a grave mistake given her lack of experience in the area.

She and Jeremy weren't an exciting couple; their relationship was more like a mending, two lives they'd lived together for so long, they just became one. Hardly a topic that would sell magazines. What *could* she write about that would help with the magazine's success and consequently her own?

Fiction isn't your strong suit, Gen. Genevieve sat back with an exasperated huff and reached into her bag for a snack. She pulled out some gummy bears and started to chew one as she brainstormed. She had promised Ms. Davies—*Harper*—a fresh perspective. She'd led her new boss to believe her background coming from a small, conservative town would add a new spin to the magazine's content, but she wasn't sure she could deliver.

People buzzed around her in the office. Through the window, she saw couples walking hand in hand down the street outside her window. Every race and sexuality was present, and eccentrically dressed individuals and men in business suits mingled along the sidewalks. Everyone was so different from her, which was scary.

Genevieve smacked herself on the forehead. The answer was so simple. All she had to do was follow through with the promise she'd made to Harper. She tossed the remainder of the candies aside and cracked a few knuckles. This time when she started typing, the words came effortlessly and honestly.

A few hours later, after several revisions and edits, Genevieve walked along the boardwalk that night considering the article she had submitted. She was proud of it, simply put. The lulling rush of the ocean's waves helped relax the tension in her shoulders. Though it had all started as a small lie, Genevieve was sure now this was the right move for her. She inhaled the sea air deeply, feeling it fuse with her spirit.

She had just written the most personal article of her career, and with that came the promise of self-discovery and sharing a life as it blossomed. The cool breeze pushed her hair away from her face as she stared at the moonlight dancing along the ocean. Genevieve explained to the readers just as she explained it to herself. It was finally time for her to grow up.

Step Four

Make Friends

Genevieve was less intimidated after surviving her first day at the office. She felt like she had found her role and was ready to settle into it. Even her desk felt more like her own when she added a few personal details, like the small cactus that had once decorated her desk at the *Sunrise*. The small, prickly greenery made Genevieve smile because it was the first plant she had managed to keep alive for longer than a week.

She grabbed a pen from a small mesh basket she got at an office supply store and started her morning brainstorming session. Genevieve jotted down a few quick ideas in her spiral notebook, and as she dotted her final *i*, she knew she'd have to get a cup of coffee before she could do anything else. She grabbed the new mug she had brought with her and rose to find Dana standing behind her. She jumped, nearly dropping it.

"Miss Applegate—"

"Please." Genevieve placed her mug back on the desk and moved her shaking hand over her racing heart. "I told you to call me Gen."

"Good morning, Gen. I'm sorry about startling you, but Ms. Davies would like to see you in her office." Genevieve wondered if she had time to make coffee first, but Dana said,

"Immediately." Genevieve looked back at the empty mug on her desk and frowned, following Dana wordlessly.

She wasn't sure if she was more worried about Harper's sudden beckoning or Dana's ninja-like skills. Genevieve could tell from the start that Harper's assistant was a spitfire and possibly the coal that kept *Out Shore*'s engine running.

Once they stopped outside Harper's office door, Dana abandoned her, leaving her to conquer the last few feet on her own. Genevieve knocked lightly and cleared her throat. Harper looked up from a stack of paperwork and smiled politely.

"Genevieve, come in and have a seat." Harper beckoned Genevieve forward and turned her attention to her bright computer screen. She squinted faintly and began to read aloud. *"With inexperienced and eager eyes, I now see the world in a new light. This light is colorful, welcoming, and beautiful in its diversity. I cannot wait to see what it has in store for me."* Harper looked away from the computer and directly at her. "That's beautiful, Genevieve."

"Thank you, I meant every word." Genevieve tugged nervously at the cuff of her maroon cardigan.

"I hope that's true, which is why I called you in here." Harper leaned forward and clasped her hands together on her desktop. Genevieve shifted nervously. "Genevieve, you've managed to do something not one other writer on my staff has done."

Genevieve's mind conjured up a hundred different possibilities, ranging from fooling Harper to alienating the entire staff. "What's that?"

Harper's gentle smile was the same one Genevieve had received during her interview and one she felt would accompany some of the happiest moments of her life. *Happiest moments of my career,* she corrected herself.

"You wrote your very first article on your very first day. There's usually a lot more trial and error involved."

"My first article?"

"You'll be published in this week's issue."

"My article?"

"Your article."

"My words?"

Harper started to laugh. "Your article that is comprised of your words, yes."

Genevieve was, for once, speechless. She expected weeks of being treated like a newbie and writing about topics assigned to her before being given this opportunity. She was an employee for all of two days and was about to be published for writing something from her heart. What kind of dream world was this?

She had to ask. "Are you sure?"

"I'm positive. You hit the nail on the head with this first piece, and I think it's exactly what this publication needs. We've managed to reach out to most of the community, but I think you'll be able to really make a difference. Just keep up the honest writing. Think you can do that?"

Genevieve took a breath as the weight of Harper's words settled in her chest. Her jaw tensed, and she struggled to keep her expression neutral. Honest writing? Make a difference? She nodded absentmindedly. The pressure of writing a cover piece about the most recent pie bake competition had nothing on this. Finally she said, "Of course."

"Great!" Harper clapped. "I won't keep you from your work any longer, but come back here at twelve. I'd like to take you out." Genevieve's eyes widened, and Harper was quick to amend, "To lunch!" Harper laughed nervously and rubbed the spot between her eyes. "I like to take new employees to lunch on their first day, but I missed yours yesterday." Harper unbuttoned her cuffs and started to roll her sleeves to mid-forearm.

"Oh, okay." Genevieve forced a stiff smile and readied herself to leave her boss's office. "See you at twelve."

She thought she had earned lunch for doing something no other employee had done, for being something special, but finding out the opposite had deflated her. Genevieve chalked her disappointment up to her tendency to overachieve and left the office as quietly as she had entered.

Genevieve walked back to her desk in a daze, but each step along the way helped clear her head. She was two days into her new job and successful thus far. This thought on loop had Genevieve smiling by time she sat in her chair.

"Don't look now, but Clarissa is on her way over," Maxine said gruffly. She sighed.

"Someone looks happy after a meeting with the boss." Clarissa leaned against the open desk space between Genevieve and Maxine, blocking the older woman from Genevieve's sight.

"I received some positive feedback," Genevieve said. She wasn't about to play games, but she also wasn't eager to appear rude to her new coworkers by ignoring them.

"I'm sure she told you how great your writing is and that you'll help make a difference." Genevieve looked up at Clarissa quickly. Her mouth fell open, but she had nothing in the way of a response. Clarissa let out a low chuckle that ended in her clucking her tongue. "You'd think she'd come up with better lines than that by now. I guess it's true what they say about old dogs." Clarissa pushed off the desk and started her retreat, but not without leaning into Genevieve's ear and whispering, "Watch out, she really likes the innocent ones." Genevieve watched Clarissa stalk away.

"Don't listen to Clarissa. She tells the same story to every woman that starts here," Maxine said.

"Why, though? What does she have to gain? I'm not after her job." Genevieve looked out the window as she contemplated her own questions. The biggest motivator for a woman to act like that would be jealousy. "Does she have a thing for Harper?" Matthew's loud cackle made her flinch.

"Yeah, Gen," he said. "Something like that." He looked at Maxine, who shared the same conspiring smile. Genevieve sat wondering how much deeper she could get herself in one day.

❖

"The coal-fired pizzas are good, but I highly recommend the Cuban sandwich." Harper leaned across the small table and pointed to the side of the menu that listed sandwiches. "All of them are good, trust me," Harper said with a wink. "I never lie about food."

"What about their salads?"

"I wouldn't know much about those. I only eat real food."

"Oh?" Genevieve's laughter continued to bubble in her throat. "I'll have to remember that."

"Good afternoon, Harper." A young waitress approached the table and placed her hand on Harper's shoulder before looking to Genevieve. "I'm Tammy, Harper's favorite waitress here." She gave Harper's shoulder a rub for good measure. The small gesture did not go unnoticed by Genevieve.

"This is Genevieve, the latest writer at *Out Shore*," Harper said, gesturing toward Genevieve. Tammy's hand never strayed far from Harper's shoulder.

"Welcome aboard." Tammy smiled at Genevieve but returned her attention to Harper instantly. "What'll it be today? Do *not* say the Cuban."

Harper hung her head guiltily.

"She's that bad?" Genevieve said, looking directly at Harper.

"Worse! Last week she came in and—"

"Okay, you two!" Harper raised her hands in defeat. "I'm pretty terrible, but I'm not *that* bad."

Genevieve picked up her menu again. "I'll have the Cuban," she said, and Harper grinned with pride. "And Harper will have whatever salad special you have." Harper stopped smiling. "You know what she likes," Genevieve said with a wink aimed at Tammy. "Surprise her."

"I like her, Harper. Give her a raise." Tammy smiled broadly and collected the menus from the table, touching Harper's shoulder again before leaving the women alone.

Harper fixed her napkin on her lap and adjusted the rolled cuffs of her shirt. She looked at Genevieve and said, "Are you always this sassy with your boss?"

Genevieve's smile fell. She never saw the line until she had already crossed it. "I'm so sorry!" Genevieve covered her face with her hands. "I always get ahead of myself and act like everyone is my friend and I make things awkward!" She peeked between her fingers and added, "I'll take the salad."

Harper sat still before she cleared her throat and repeated, "I don't eat salads."

Genevieve squirmed in her seat, not catching the teasing lilt of Harper's voice. "I know," she said with a groan. "You said that and I blatantly disregarded it." Genevieve covered her face again and Harper stopped her by gently grasping her forearm.

"It's okay, really," Harper said. Her gentle laugh helped relieve some of the tension twisting the muscles between Genevieve's shoulders. "I prefer having friendly relationships with my writers—teasing, hanging out, and sharing life stories, the whole nine yards." Harper released Genevieve's arm and sat back with a faux puff of confidence broadening her chest. "Hey, maybe it's time for me to try something new."

Genevieve's mood shifted instantly and she grinned. "I'm sure you'll love whatever *Tammy* brings you."

Harper shook her head. "I don't know what you're talking about."

"Oh please!" Genevieve leaned forward and laid her hand on Harper's shoulder. She was immediately struck by the firm muscle she felt beneath her fingertips. "She knows exactly what you like," she said in a mock purr.

"Of course she does, I've been coming here for years!" Harper's defense was weak.

"Hmmm." She picked up her ice water and took a long sip, the clattering of the ice cubes the only sound at the table. She placed the glass back in its small wet ring. "How many times has she asked you out?"

Harper's initial response was a comical noise, something between a scoff and a squawk.

Genevieve arched one eyebrow as she assessed her boss from across the table. "How many times, Harper?"

Harper shook her head and rolled her eyes. "Four, maybe five? I don't know. I wasn't counting."

Genevieve opened her mouth and closed it immediately. She worried her lower lip between her teeth as she considered her response. She had already crossed one line, but her curiosity was gnawing at her. Her face twisted painfully.

"Just say it, Genevieve." Harper adjusted her napkin again and looked up at Genevieve through her dark lashes.

"Have you ever accepted?"

"And risk losing one of my favorite places to eat? Never."

They both sat back as lunch was served moments later. Before Genevieve had the chance to bite into her sandwich,

Harper leaned forward and said, "That sandwich is worth turning down a date, I promise." She sat back and prepared her salad, with a little help from Genevieve, and the two women fell into a companionable silence as they ate.

Once Harper's salad was half its original size and Genevieve had the chance to enjoy most of her sandwich with few interruptions, Harper started to talk business. She brought up key points of Genevieve's first installment and mentioned what she'd like to see in future issues. Eventually, the topic melded with Genevieve's personal life.

"The more personal you get, the better." Harper took a final bite of her food and chewed slowly. After she swallowed, she said, "If this becomes a steady column, your topics are limitless, really. I can offer you a lot of direction, but I need to know something first." Harper wiped her mouth.

"What's that?"

"Do you have a partner?"

Genevieve froze mid-bite. "Partner?"

"I'm sorry, I know some people don't prefer that term, and since you're not wearing a ring I'll ask, do you have a girlfriend?" Harper waited for an answer, but as Genevieve chewed slowly, she continued. "Anyone you left behind in Pennsylvania?" Harper watched Genevieve continue to chew. "You're a slow eater."

"It's healthier." Genevieve laughed stiffly. "No girlfriend, no partner." She sat back and fiddled with the napkin on her lap. "There's someone in Pennsylvania, but..." She looked out the large front windows and squinted slightly at the bright sunlight.

Harper tilted her head. "But what?"

In an instant, Genevieve had a newfound clarity. A feeling that had lain dormant, hidden beneath routine comfort, surfaced with a breathtaking realization. "But I think I may have outgrown it." She had never admitted that to anyone, not even herself.

Harper nodded. "Good."

"Excuse me?"

"Good for the magazine!" Harper grimaced. "That doesn't sound much better. What I'm trying to say is that if you're single, you can write about navigating the dating scene. Dating and relationships are always hot topics, and our readers will root for you. It'll be like tuning in to their favorite TV show week after week."

Genevieve swallowed. "Dating…"

"If you're ready to date, that is," Harper said with a sigh. "I'm sorry."

"For what?"

"Pushing you like this. I just get a little excitable when something new happens at *Out Shore*. I just compared your life to a TV show."

"It's okay, Harper." Genevieve let out a strangled laugh. Her plate was empty, so she pushed it aside and focused on Harper. She needed to deflect, and turning the tables on her boss seemed like the best way to do just that. "What about you? Also no ring." Genevieve pointed to Harper's left hand. "Single, or do you have a partner?"

"I'm in a long-term relationship with *Out Shore* at the moment." Something about the way she said it bothered Genevieve, but she couldn't quite figure out why.

"That's surprising."

"Why?" Harper said with a smirk.

"It just is," Genevieve said, looking thoughtful for a moment. "You just don't look like someone who'd be single often or for long."

Harper sat up taller. "Well, if that's what we're basing these things on, then I'll say you won't be single much longer."

Genevieve blushed and tucked a strand of hair behind her ear.

"Can I get you anything else?" Tammy said from beside the table.

"I think we're good." Harper looked at her watch, and her eyes widened. "We should be heading back. I may be the boss, but it's bad business to keep people from getting their work done." Harper paid the bill and waited for Genevieve to gather her things before making her way to the door.

Genevieve spoke quietly as they walked back to the office. "Thank you for lunch. This whole transition and experience has been easy and welcoming."

"I'm very happy to hear that."

"Did you like your salad?" she said.

"It was very good!"

"You ate everything but the lettuce."

"Like I said, it was very good." Harper chuckled when Genevieve rolled her eyes and started to walk away.

STEP FIVE

Listen to Those Around You

G enevieve was an instant success. Each weekly installment she wrote gained more attention than the last, which pleased both Genevieve and Harper immensely. Harper never shied away from sharing her outward excitement with Genevieve, whether it was by stopping at her desk to read a particularly shining email from a reader or acknowledging Genevieve's numbers in an office meeting. The attention made Genevieve giddy. She just liked impressing her boss; that's what she told herself, anyway. Harper Davies seemed like the type of boss who was quick to be proud of her staff, but equally hard to impress.

She also made new friends. A few of her coworkers had made it a habit to invite Genevieve along to any and all of their planned shenanigans, citing both a fun night and guaranteed material for her next column. Genevieve would often decline, preferring to head home and put on sweatpants before opening a beer and working on a blog post or clearing out her DVR. She already had enough potential material thanks to the heart of her column being a lie.

Genevieve sat back from her desk with a sigh and readjusted her thick-rimmed glasses. She stretched her back and rubbed at the tension brewing at the base of her spine. The enormity of her lie weighed on her shoulders every day, but Genevieve tried to focus on the positive. She was flourishing in her new role and she had managed to keep the extent of her lies to a minimum. She looked at her spiral notebook and scanned the ideas she had for upcoming issues. Near the bottom, circled in red, was the one idea that scared her most, but this topic was also the one that *Out Shore* and her readers would have to see eventually: *Go on a <u>DATE</u>.* She popped a gummy bear in her mouth and chewed nervously.

Would that be so hard? Genevieve mulled the idea over. *Go out with a woman and simply enjoy her company?* They could have a few drinks and chat amicably about their lives. That didn't sound like a difficult feat at all. Hell, Genevieve had always enjoyed the company of her girlfriends over the boys since childhood. Genevieve smiled as she remembered all the games of make-believe she'd participated in. More than once, she had insisted a household would be better off with two mommies anyway, so an innocent date should be easy.

"It's such a turn-off when they don't breathe." Genevieve heard Clarissa over the quiet music she was listening to through earbuds. She pulled one out in order to hear more clearly. "I mean come on, I'm looking for an orgasm, not to get you into the *Guinness Book of World Records*!"

Genevieve turned her chair just enough to watch Clarissa's movements out of the corner of her eye. Clarissa had draped herself across the corner of Maxine's desk as they chatted amicably. Clarissa, as Genevieve had come to learn over the past few weeks, was friendly with everyone else in the office, and in charge of sex and relationships, something she reminded Genevieve of every time her column even touched on the topic. Genevieve couldn't wait to write a piece about dating just to get under Clarissa's skin.

"I was with a girl once who was a heavy-duty mouth breather, both in *and* out of the bedroom," Maxine said with a shake of her head. "Imagine a leaf blower between your legs." Clarissa laughed, and Genevieve found herself becoming irrationally annoyed at the beautiful sight. *Why are the mean girls always so attractive?*

Clarissa patted Maxine's shoulder as she shuddered at the memory. "It couldn't have been that bad, Max. If I'm ever with someone who doesn't know what they're doing, I just make sure I tell them exactly what I need them to do. I may come across bossy," Clarissa said, waving her hand flippantly, "but I always come."

"I always come," Genevieve said under her breath, mocking Clarissa's voice. She turned back to her work and sugary snack. Her pen had hit the paper for no more than two seconds before Clarissa asked her next question.

"What's your signature move?"

"What makes you think I have a signature move?" Maxine said.

"You've been married for seventeen years! You have to have some tricks up your sleeve to keep things lively for that long." Genevieve didn't have to look at Clarissa to know she was wearing a salacious smile.

"Fine, but I swear to God, Clarissa, if you tell my wife I said any of this..." Genevieve drew closer. Clarissa must've nodded in agreement because Maxine started to whisper. "I wait a little while. You know, once the touching and caressing becomes too much and too little at the same time? Then..." Maxine's voice dropped even more, but Genevieve needed to know. She'd like to bring this information back to Jeremy.

Genevieve leaned back in her chair, picking up the next bit of Maxine's seduction techniques, but the wheels beneath her chair gave out and she fell backward onto the floor with a less-than-discreet squeal. She looked up into Maxine's concerned, flushed face and Clarissa's overly amused smirk.

"What about you, Gen? Do you have any moves, or wait—let me guess. You're a pillow princess, aren't you?" Clarissa's sneer was just as dangerous from Genevieve's position on the floor. Genevieve had no idea what a pillow princess was, but context clues led her to believe it was intended as an insult. She scoffed as she jumped to her feet and righted her chair.

"I am not, I mean, I uh…"

"Leave the poor girl alone, Clarissa," Maxine said, "and get back to work."

Genevieve watched as Clarissa sauntered away, waiting for her to reach a safe distance before talking to Maxine again. "I don't get it. When is she going to leave me alone?"

"Relax, Gen, it'll happen. You're the first young female hire in a while that threatens her status as the hottest thing at *Out Shore*."

Genevieve was confused. "But I thought Matthew said Harper hasn't hired any men lately."

"Hunks," Maxine said. "The last men Harper hired were either married or not Matthew's type, and the last woman was older than me."

Genevieve looked over her shoulder nonchalantly enough to not get caught staring at Clarissa and the way she laughed with another writer. "I'm not saying I want to be her friend, but I do wish she'd realize I'm not here to take anything from her. I want us all to be successful."

"I know you do, Gen, and I'm sure deep down Clarissa does, too." Maxine turned back to her computer. "Soon enough she'll come around, and you'll be sharing your latest sex-capades with her, too."

Trading sex stories with Clarissa? Genevieve's chest tightened at the idea. "I need some air."

Genevieve excused herself and made her way for the door. She needed fresh air to cool down because she was embarrassed and pissed off. Genevieve stepped out onto the sidewalk and paused as soon as the doors behind her closed. She pushed her glasses to the top of her head and looked up. Genevieve smiled toward the sunshine. She welcomed the way the chill of October cut through the material of her sweater and teased her heated skin. She wondered how long Clarissa planned to torture her as a new hire.

"Hey!"

Genevieve heard a voice call out, but she kept her face turned toward the sky with her eyes closed. There were many voices around her on the street, why pay any attention to this one?

"Genevieve?"

Harper was seated on a bench beside her. Genevieve couldn't keep the smile from blossoming across her face.

"Harper! What brings you to the sidewalk on such a lovely afternoon?" Genevieve looked at Harper, no longer in awe of the sunshine's beauty.

"Fresh air and a snack." She held up a small bag of potato chips. "What about you?" Harper asked, motioning to the empty space beside her. "Join me."

"I suppose the same." Genevieve sat at the other end of the bench. The sun did wonders for Harper's eyes, turning their deep pewter highlights to navy. Genevieve saw such softness, such kindness in those eyes that she found herself wanting to tell Harper all about the incident with Clarissa. But she reminded herself Harper was her boss, and she'd more than likely defend a senior member of her staff. She kept it simple.

"Sometimes I just need a moment to breathe." Genevieve took a deep breath to prove her point.

"I hope your first month is going well. Everyone is being welcoming, yes?"

Genevieve closed her eyes momentarily. Harper's question went beyond simple manners. She was genuinely concerned, like she knew about the particular struggles Genevieve was facing.

She smiled softly before saying, "Yes, I already feel more comfortable here than I did at the *Sunrise*. And I was there for years!"

"I'm sure it helps that you're surrounded by people like you."

Genevieve furrowed her brow in confusion.

"Lesbians," Harper said with a chuckle.

"Oh, right." Genevieve swallowed hard. Sometimes she forgot certain details of her new life. "That is certainly a big help." Genevieve focused on her hands, folded together on her lap.

Harper turned the bag of chips she'd been holding in Genevieve's direction. "Want one?" Harper's offer was so small, but Genevieve warmed to it immediately.

"I shouldn't. I give up junk food every winter. Everything except gummy bears—they don't hibernate." Genevieve laughed at her small, poor joke.

"I don't think I could survive without snacking." Harper looked serious as she considered this and ate another potato chip. The loud crunching filled the space between them. "No, I really wouldn't."

Genevieve chortled. "Someone likes to exaggerate," she said playfully, smiling at Harper. Genevieve noted the way Harper's tailored suit pants hugged her frame perfectly. She looked like a woman who enjoyed the gym. Her black oxford shirt clung to her thick upper arms and broad shoulders. *How did this body come from a need for snacking?* "I don't believe you." When Genevieve's eyes finally met Harper's, she realized she seemed to be checking her out. She blushed and bit her lip.

"Believe it, Genevieve. To answer your next question, yes, I work out and no, I don't enjoy it. But if it means more chips and candy..." Harper ate another chip and smirked.

"Fair trade-off?" Genevieve said, and Harper nodded. Genevieve stared blankly across the street once they fell silent. She tried to focus on the air around her and the comfort of the moment, but she wanted Harper to keep talking. Her gentle voice helped erase the unease Clarissa had wedged into her chest, and the way Harper looked at her made Genevieve feel butterflies in her stomach for the first time in years. She shifted uncomfortably. Where were these thoughts coming from? And more importantly, where were they leading?

"Are you sure you're okay?" Harper said in a voice much firmer than usual.

Genevieve jumped slightly and laughed off the concern. "Yeah, definitely. Just been staring at a computer screen for too long. That's actually why I wear these." Genevieve removed the glasses from atop her head. "My mother insisted I see an eye doctor after getting one too many headaches. I didn't need a prescription, but as it turns out they make lenses for people like me who live on their computer."

Genevieve ran her fingertip along the frame of her glasses and smiled at the memory of her mother's worry. "Mom still thinks computers will fry my brain, but I can think of worse ways to go. Like never snacking again."

Harper gasped dramatically. They shared a laugh, and

Harper stared back at Genevieve with the slightest smile. Genevieve wanted to squirm under the attention, but she also never wanted it to end.

"Tell me more about your family," Harper said.

Genevieve took a breath. "The short or the long version?"

"You decide."

"I'm the middle child, sandwiched between two boys. They followed in my father's footsteps and joined the Navy right out of high school. When I mentioned wanting to do the same, I was told that the military is for men." Genevieve shrugged off Harper's scowl. "I was diagnosed with a heart murmur my junior year of high school." Genevieve leaned in closer. "I tell my mom it's the only reason why I didn't enlist against her wishes, but that was also around the time I realized I'd never survive in the Navy, or in any branch of the military, for that matter."

Harper laughed, loudly and openly, and Genevieve felt an odd sense of pride swell at the effect she was having on her.

"Is your family back in Pennsylvania?"

"My mom and brothers are, yes. We lived there my whole life. No matter where my dad was stationed, she stayed with us in Pennsylvania so we'd have some semblance of normalcy." Genevieve reached across the small space between her and Harper and took a chip. She put the whole thing in her mouth and chewed before saying, "That definitely helped my dad hide his affairs."

Harper's mouth fell open, the same reaction Genevieve received from most people when she told this story. She couldn't hold back her giggle. "They divorced when I was ten. It was for the best."

Harper placed the bag of chips on the bench and started to wipe her hands off. Genevieve waited for her to look at her again, to continue her story, but Harper's whole demeanor had changed.

"The three of us wanted out of Milan so badly." Genevieve continued through the awkwardness, hopeful she could undo the damage she had done to the moment. "But I was the only one who made it out." She was overwhelmed with the need to reach out and physically grab Harper's attention once more. Genevieve placed a gentle hand on Harper's shoulder and said, "I think I wound up right where I'm supposed to be."

Harper looked first at Genevieve's hand and then at Genevieve before her face melted into a broad grin. "I do, too." Genevieve's smile matched Harper's instantly, and they sat in silence for a moment more before Harper said, "I'm keeping you from your work again. I seem to be making this a bad habit."

Harper stood, prompting Genevieve to do the same. She stepped forward and opened the door for Genevieve, ushering her inside with a small touch to her lower back. "Enjoy the rest of your afternoon, Genevieve." Harper made her way to her office, leaving Genevieve alone in the heart of the bustling space.

Genevieve took in the people around her, the woman who had just left her, and all the possibilities that lay before her. Her career was just getting started, but she already had a following, her coworkers were *mostly* great, and her boss was... Genevieve looked to Harper's open office door. Harper Davies was wonderful.

One year, Genevieve thought. *One year of keeping my story straight.* She laughed at the unintentional pun. *I'll get a year of experience under my belt for my resume and then I'll quit. If anyone asks, I fell for a person, Jeremy, who was a man and an exception. That happens, right?* She nodded definitively. The first month was already wrapping up. She'd only have to keep lying for eleven more.

Motion from the corner of her eye caught Genevieve's attention. Harper stood just inside her office, talking on the phone. Her broad, vibrant smile captured Genevieve's focus fully. She sighed, praying eleven months would pass easily.

Step Six

Have a Confidante

With so many different eateries, bars, and eclectic shops, weekend activities in Asbury Park were plentiful and guaranteed fun. However, Genevieve found weekends to be the perfect time to indulge in sweatpants, country music, beer, and being home alone. Genevieve rarely experienced this kind of quiet solitude back in Pennsylvania. If Jeremy wasn't stopping by unexpectedly, her best friend, Chloe, would surely be showing up with a grand plan for them.

Genevieve sat in her home office and closed her eyes. She relished the way her music echoed in her silent apartment. When she opened her eyes, she looked down at her open notebook and smiled in satisfaction at the notes scribbled along the margins and Post-its sticking out from between the pages. She needed this time to focus on keeping her column believable as well as consistent, and to work on her side job of freelance blog posting.

She opened to a page with a starred Post-it attached, listing off event web pages that detailed every different singles mixer, ladies' night, and potential matchmaking event taking place in town that month. Genevieve entertained the idea of venturing out to one that night, but as she shifted and felt the soft fleece lining of her pants rub against her legs, she knew this was not the weekend she'd be meeting new people. She turned the page and tapped her finger along to the twang of a banjo.

Pillow Princess. She had written the words in red and traced over them several times to make sure they were bold enough to bleed through to the other side of the page. Genevieve grimaced when Clarissa's face came into her mind. She turned to her computer and opened Google. "What is a pillow princess?" She spoke the words as she typed them and hit enter. Once the first result loaded, she read the description aloud: "*A woman, usually in a curious/bisexual context, who wants to experience pleasure from oral sex, but who is unwilling to reciprocate.*" Genevieve sat back with her mouth agape. "I am *not* a pillow princess!"

As soon as the sting of Clarissa's words started to wear off, Genevieve realized being insulted was silly because that definition didn't apply to her. She barely even experienced pleasure from oral sex. Genevieve's face fell. If she was going to make it through a year as a lesbian, she'd need to figure out a thing or two about being with women, and that included increasing her sexual knowledge. She pulled her hair back into a loose bun and started typing again.

Sex with Jeremy wasn't exactly bad, though it was vanilla and the same thing for nearly ten years. No matter how many suggestions she had made or new ideas she tried to bring into the bedroom, he wasn't on board. She met any idea he had with enthusiasm, but it usually ended with her dissatisfaction as well.

Genevieve considered her present situation alongside her past. *What if I invited another woman into the bedroom?* She nearly choked on her laughter and spoke to herself. "Definitely not."

Her first search was for lesbian sex tips. The first three pages of results were nothing more than porn. She grabbed another beer and took a few sips before deciding to just click on the first video that appealed to her. The scene was a sleepover between friends. Genevieve laughed at the cliché, but she hit play anyway.

Two blondes shared a bed and were dressed in the same barely-there pajama set. They wore pink thongs and too-tiny white T-shirts. They were "asleep" for the first five seconds of the video before one of them cracked open an overly lined and shadowed eye to look over at her bedmate. *Okay,* Genevieve thought, *this isn't so bad.* Genevieve almost choked on her mouthful of beer when the woman who was wide awake started to masturbate next to her costar. Predictably, the other woman awoke and things escalated quickly.

"Wow, okay," Genevieve said as she took in their artificially large breasts, a lot of tongue action, and *very* long nails going places they shouldn't. She closed one eye when one stubborn string of saliva wouldn't leave a woman's chin, but continued watching as the other woman thrashed with the most over-acted orgasm Genevieve had ever seen. Genevieve had faked better orgasms herself, and she hadn't gotten paid for them. She closed her browser and finished her beer. Judging by the results of this research, the rest of Genevieve's year at *Out Shore* would be more difficult than expected. Genevieve was *definitely* straight.

❖

Genevieve walked into work with a new sense of confidence thanks to her research-filled weekend. After the porn disaster, Genevieve went to a local bookstore and stocked up on books about lesbian relationships and every LGBT-themed magazine she could get her hands on. Combined with the back issues of *Out Shore* she had been collecting, Genevieve had plenty of material.

Mondays had a unique energy in the *Out Shore* office. Final drafts had to be submitted by Wednesday, and most writers were rushing around to solidify topics and getting final approval from trusted coworkers. Genevieve was finishing up the outline she had been working on since Friday. This week's installment would be about integrating old friends into your new life, something Genevieve had yet to do. But she planned on calling Chloe that night to let her in on her latest situation. Saying that she was in need of a levelheaded perspective would be an understatement.

Genevieve was preparing her second cup of coffee in the break room when Clarissa walked in with Matthew. He was a delight to be around when alone, but he became loud and incorrigible with Clarissa around.

"All I'm saying is that this magazine needs more spice." Clarissa was talking as usual. Genevieve rolled her eyes.

"And I'm willing to bet you're the perfect candidate for that job?" Matthew's question was obviously rhetorical, but Clarissa answered anyway.

"Of course! Who else would be?"

Genevieve started to bristle, knowing she'd find herself at the butt of yet another Clarissa attack if she didn't get out of there quickly.

"Who would you pick?" Clarissa said to Matthew. "Maxine, myself, or Prudence over here?" Genevieve turned slowly.

Matthew held back a laugh, and Clarissa smiled proudly. Genevieve wanted to be witty and quick with a scalding response, but confrontation never came naturally to her, so the best she could muster up was a simple, "Ha ha, Clarissa. Good one."

Genevieve turned away, but something about Clarissa's snickering got beneath her skin. She looked back over her shoulder while walking away. "And by the way, I'm *not* a pillow princess!" She almost ran into Harper standing there, and she spilled her coffee all over her own front.

Genevieve's face reddened. Before Harper could say anything, Genevieve ran for the bathroom. She grabbed as many paper towels as she could hold and soaked them with water. Less than a minute into her sink bath, Harper entered the bathroom. Genevieve looked up from her damaged clothes to find Harper looking on in concern.

"I assure you," Genevieve said over the running faucet, "I'm always this clumsy." Genevieve continued to scrub her shirt as she spoke. "I've learned to buy at least two of all my favorite pieces of clothing because I'll ruin one." When Harper didn't respond, Genevieve looked up. She leaned against the counter with her arms folded across her chest, and her smile matched the softness in her eyes. Genevieve saw the question in them before Harper even spoke it. "I'm fine."

"Is Clarissa giving you a hard time?" When Genevieve didn't answer, Harper shook her head. "I should've known. She's usually at the heart of any office drama." Harper grabbed a few more paper towels and handed them to Genevieve. "I can't apologize enough."

"You have nothing to apologize for. Every workplace has a bully."

"I don't want my workplace to have one, and deep down, I don't think Clarissa wants to be one," Harper said with a sigh. "I can't fire her because she never really crosses the line into rightful termination, and she won't work from home."

"Working from home sounds nice," Genevieve mused

aloud as she worked on a particularly large coffee spot on her thigh.

"That's not an option for you." Harper's voice was stern, but her smile was playful. "We'd miss having you around the office."

"Oh, would we?" Genevieve found herself flirting, and Harper's widening smile encouraged her to continue. "I find that hard to believe."

Harper winked. "Believe it, Genevieve. Run home for a change of clothes. I'll cover for you with the boss."

Genevieve watched in amusement as Harper snuck out of the bathroom like she was keeping a secret. She giggled and looked back at her reflection. She was blushing profusely. Genevieve touched her warm cheeks before fanning her face. The source of the flush could be either embarrassment or... Genevieve looked back to the closed door and replayed Harper's wink one more time. Her stomach fluttered instantly.

"Embarrassment it is." Genevieve cleared her throat and looked around the empty restroom. She cleaned up the pile of paper towels and threw them out before heading home to change like Harper suggested.

As Genevieve entered her apartment, she dialed Chloe. "Hey!" she said the moment the ringing stopped.

"Well hello, Gen. I was beginning to think you had forgotten about me." Chloe's warm voice soothed Genevieve's still-addled nerves.

"Nonsense and impossible. You know that," Genevieve said, starting to take off her soiled clothing. "How have you been?"

"Bored without you, but managing. More importantly, how are *you* doing? Judging by my lack of mail, you still haven't subscribed me to your magazine." Chloe had been texting Genevieve regularly, begging for copies of her work, online links, and subscriptions, which Genevieve had ignored as she tried to work out an explanation to give.

"I'll send you a few back issues this week, and I'll have you subscribed by Friday." Genevieve pulled on a pair of clean jeans. After that morning's incident, she was heading back to the office much more casual.

Chloe sighed dramatically into the phone. "I don't believe you."

"Believe it, because I'm finally ready to tell you about my job. And you haven't tried to search me online, right? You promised."

"I've upheld my promise and so has Jeremy, surprisingly."

"He didn't search anything because he really doesn't care." Genevieve shrugged on a sweater and felt a little sad at the truth of the statement. Jeremy didn't care. He made it clear by their nightly phone calls that all he cared about was not having her around.

"He still hasn't shown much support, has he?"

"No, and he doesn't even try to ask me about it." Genevieve checked her hair and light makeup in a small mirror. "Last night we were on the phone for fifteen minutes before he asked me to have phone sex, followed by him asking when I was coming home next. He didn't like either answer, so he ended our conversation because he was tired."

"You know how he is. If it's not about Jeremy, then Jeremy doesn't care."

Genevieve shook her head solemnly. "It'd be nice if he acted like he cared for a change."

"He's been this way since high school. I'm surprised it took you this long to get tired of it."

"Maybe it's just because I actually have something exciting happening for me—"

"Then tell me all about it! I've been dying over here!"

Genevieve smiled at her friend's support. Chloe had always been right beside Genevieve throughout their lives, even when it came to the craziest of her plans.

Genevieve took a deep breath. "Well, it all started with a job listing that I read a little too quickly before hitting the 'apply now' button." Chloe already started to laugh.

Genevieve recounted everything from how she got the job to why she was home in the middle of the afternoon changing her clothes. She wrapped up the tale just as she arrived back at the office. She stood outside the building and waited for Chloe to give her some sort of advice.

"Oh my God, Gen." Chloe was breathless with laughter by the time Genevieve finished. "This is, by far, the most ridiculous thing you've ever done!" Chloe's cackle hurt Genevieve's ear, and she pulled the phone away.

"Like I didn't know that already," Genevieve nearly growled. "I'm telling you this so you can help me."

"Help you? Sweetie, no one can help you now."

"Thank you, Chloe, I knew I could count on you," Genevieve said, checking her watch. "I have to get back to work,"

"Okay, listen, call me later, and we'll figure this out—"

Genevieve chortled and stopped Chloe. "Easier said than done."

"Being a lady-lover will come naturally to you, trust me. I love you and we'll talk later. Good-bye, Gen." Chloe hung up a second later, leaving Genevieve to wonder exactly why her best friend had so much confidence in her.

STEP SEVEN

Use Your Imagination

Genevieve loved autumn. The changing of leaves and some of the best holidays took place then. She relished the gorgeous New Jersey sunsets, regardless of how early they started. She really enjoyed the evening, when the office was near empty and she could just enjoy the view. The pinks and oranges stretched out across the sky over the city. Genevieve sat at her desk with a head full of ideas and thoughts of the previous weekend she had spent back in Pennsylvania.

She had gone to surprise her mother, Sandra, and placate Jeremy's constant nagging that she never made time to see him. Genevieve tried to point out he didn't make an effort to see her either, but he was deaf to the point. She had put together a game night like they used to have every week, with Genevieve, Jeremy, Sandra, Chloe, and whomever Chloe was dating at the time. Chloe had arrived solo that night, much to Genevieve's delight. She needed the ease and familiarity of home and quality time with her best friend. What should've been a relaxing night turned out to be anything but.

"My vote is for Scattergories," Genevieve said as she twisted the top off her beer.

Jeremy took the beer from her hand and kissed her head. "You always suggest Scattergories."

"That was my b—"

"I think we should play poker." Jeremy took a long pull from her beer. Genevieve narrowed her eyes. If a look could shatter glass...

"Typical guy," Chloe said as she handed Genevieve a beer with an apologetic look. "I agree with Gen, Scattergories sounds fun."

"Mom, you decide." Genevieve turned to her mother, who stood in the doorway of the kitchen as the rest of them settled at the round table in the middle of the room. Sandra was short and stocky with a head full of coppery curls, a trait Genevieve always wished she had inherited. She was a teenager before she came to terms with her natural strawberry hue. She pulled at her long, straight ponytail and waited for her mother's decision.

Sandra made a show of scratching her chin before agreeing with her daughter. "Scattergories it is. I'll go get it."

Jeremy grumbled and Genevieve pumped her fist in the air.

"You're staying over my place tonight, right?" Jeremy said while scrolling through his phone and drinking his beer.

Genevieve tugged a little harder at the end of her hair. "I planned on staying here, actually. It'll make my mom happy." Jeremy made a show out of putting his phone down, and Genevieve knew he was going to give her a hard time. "It's the last farmer's market tomorrow, and she wanted to head out early."

"I haven't seen you in over a month, Gen. Doesn't that matter to you?"

"Of course it matters." Genevieve looked over to Chloe in a silent apology for the uncomfortable scene. "But I have to make time for everyone."

"Just not me."

"You could come see me, you know." Genevieve ignored Chloe's small chuckle beside her. Sure, having Jeremy come to Asbury wouldn't be ideal considering her sort of double life, but she was arguing out of principle at this point.

"You know that's hard for me with my schedule."

"And you think it's easy with mine?"

Jeremy laughed then and Genevieve wondered how mad her mother would be if she threw her beer at him. "You can write from anywhere. Last time I checked, laptops and notebooks are portable." He was handsome, but when he smiled cockily Genevieve was appalled by him.

Before she could respond, her mother walked back in and triumphantly placed the game in the center of the table. "It wasn't easy, but I found it." Sandra looked around the quiet table. "Did you decide on teams while I was gone?"

"Yeah, Gen, did you pick your team?" Chloe smirked around the mouth of her bottle.

Genevieve shook her head at Chloe's lack of subtlety. "Ready to destroy them?"

❖

"What are you still doing here?" Genevieve nearly jumped out of her chair at the sudden voice. She spun around to see Harper standing with her hands up in the air. "I'm so sorry."

"It's okay." Genevieve brushed the hair back from her face and felt her heart racing in her chest. "I guess I just got lost in my daydreams."

Harper smiled that pleasantly soft smile Genevieve had come to know as the prelude to some outrageously sweet and caring comment. "I hope they were good daydreams."

"Hardly." Genevieve grumbled quietly before noticing Harper's jacket and briefcase. She looked at her watch and realized it was after eight o'clock. "Holy sh—moly." She grimaced at Harper. "I didn't realize it was so late."

"Did you eat?"

Genevieve was sheepish to admit how extensive her lapse in time was. "Not since lunchtime."

"Have dinner with me," Harper said. "Unless you have other plans." She didn't ask, and Genevieve was both startled and relieved by that. But then she wondered why Harper would want to have dinner with her.

"You want me to have dinner with you?" Genevieve's mind raced. Her undeniably attractive boss had just asked her to dinner. She wasn't prepared for the possibility of being asked out, and now that was happening. Why did it have to be the one person she absolutely could not be asked out by? Harper was the wrong person for so many reasons.

"Yes. I'm reviewing a new restaurant that just opened in the neighborhood and would love a second opinion."

"A work date?" Genevieve said, still a little confused by the whole proposal. Harper nodded. "I still don't know my way around that well, but I'll follow you?"

"Let's go."

❖

"This place is beautiful!" Genevieve said after she settled into a large wooden booth across from Harper.

"It is." Harper looked around. "It's also brand new, so they want to make a great first impression."

"Well, they have done that with me." Genevieve placed her linen napkin on her lap as their host took their drink order. To Genevieve's dismay, she was prompted to order first. This triggered an inner war. She was with her classy, mature boss in a swanky new restaurant that surely did not serve Budweiser. "I'll have a glass of red wine?"

The host stared blankly for a moment before asking, "What kind?"

Genevieve looked to Harper for help, but she was reading the drink menu. "It's been a long day, I'll take anything." Genevieve tried to play off the joke with a small laugh.

"Of course." The young man turned to Harper, "And for you?"

Harper smiled politely. "I'll have any lager you have on tap." Genevieve closed her eyes and fought against the urge to smack her own forehead. "Notice how we're the only ones here?" Harper said. "It's risky to open a new place in the off-season."

"You'd think they'd close earlier."

"That would make sense, but my guess is that they want to try to get as much business as possible." Harper shrugged. "So, what's your first impression?"

She was just about to speak when their waiter set their drinks down in front of them.

"My name is Eric, and I'll be your server this evening. Are you ready to order?"

"We'll take one each of your appetizers and specials, please." Harper handed their unopened menus back to Eric, who looked a bit dumbfounded.

"One of each?"

"Yes, thank you." When Eric walked away from the table, Harper looked at Genevieve and said, "That never gets old."

Genevieve laughed loudly. She was charmed by Harper's humor and playfulness. "I hope they offer doggie bags."

"It's hard to write a review if you only try one thing." Harper sipped her beer, giving the taste a moment of thought before sipping one more time. "The beer is good, how's the wine?"

Genevieve looked to the bulbous glass she had been ignoring. She smiled stiffly before lifting it to her nose. She read in one of her mother's magazines that you're supposed to sniff your wine first, for whatever reason. The smell did little to entice her. Genevieve held up her glass to Harper before going in for her first taste. She cringed. She actually cringed at the tart taste. The best she could do was hold back a shiver. To Genevieve's surprise, Harper laughed.

"Should I tell people to stay away from the reds?"

"I don't like wine," Genevieve said, covering her face with her hands. "I want to because wine culture is so sophisticated and mature!" By the time she lowered her hands, Harper had switched their drinks.

"Sometimes you have to grow to appreciate wine." Harper sipped the wine and seemed satisfied enough. "Do you like beer?"

A thrilling shiver traveled to the base of Genevieve's spine when she looked at the rim of the frosty pint glass and noticed a droplet of beer clinging to the spot Harper had drunk from. At first she sipped politely, but then she gulped the lager to erase not just the aftertaste of the wine, but the thought of Harper's mouth. "Very much," She licked the remnants of foam from her upper lip.

"Good, then leave the wine to us older folks."

"You talk like you're my mom's age." Genevieve rolled her eyes playfully.

"I'm nearly a decade older than you. That's a whole lifetime."

"Hardly!" Genevieve sat back. The beer was settling into her muscles and bones nicely. She looked across at Harper, who had her hands folded on the tabletop and was tapping her fingers together. "You want my initial thoughts on this place?"

Harper's eyes lit up. "Absolutely."

"It'd be a wonderful spot for a first date." Genevieve started to twirl a strand of her hair around her finger. "With the lighting and the privacy provided by the high-backed booths, the ambience is very romantic."

Genevieve could see it all: Harper doting on a beautiful woman, giving her date undivided attention as she spoke. They'd feed each other various delicacies and maybe even share a kiss in the candlelight. Genevieve blushed and looked at Harper's hands again. She imagined the soft skin of her palm as she held her date's hand on the tabletop. The Harper in Genevieve's mind was so attentive, she'd have her date wrapped around her finger by the end of the night.

"What's that smile about?"

Harper's question pulled Genevieve back to the moment. Maybe the beer or the comfortable, dim lighting was to blame, but Genevieve was relaxed enough to answer honestly. "I was just imagining you on a date, wooing a beautiful woman until she was putty in your hands."

Harper laughed heartily. "Are you sure you're not a fiction writer? Because you have a very active imagination."

"I may have heard you're quite the ladies'...well, lady. Especially with new hires."

"That was a long time ago."

"When was the last time you were on a date?" Genevieve said. "A *real* date."

"It's been a while," Harper said, and her avoidance intrigued Genevieve. "What about you?" She took a long drink of her wine. "Since Pennsylvania, I mean."

Genevieve wanted to answer without lying more than she

already had. "After leaving my high school sweetheart behind, I've been taking my time with getting back into the dating game." Harper didn't react. Their food arrived, and Genevieve breathed a sigh of relief, thinking the conversation was over.

Harper took charge of plating, making sure Genevieve had a little bit of everything she had ordered, but she was careful to check on Genevieve's food preferences.

"Is there anything here you're not interested in trying?"

Genevieve looked at the endless array of meat, seafood, pasta, and every vegetable New Jersey was capable of producing in the autumn. Genevieve's mouth watered. She looked up at Harper, who was still poised with her fork and knife over a platter, and shook her head. She wanted to try it all. Harper handed her an overfilled plate, and they dug into their dinner robustly without a word.

"Was leaving your sweetheart behind hard for you?" Harper said between bites of pasta.

"No." Genevieve shocked herself because the answer didn't even require a thought "That was part of my old life." She sipped her beer, swallowing back the bitter taste that accompanied that truth. "I outgrew that life, but they were settled in it. They didn't even entertain the idea of moving here with me." She pushed food around her plate.

"Would it have made a difference if she did?" For the first time that night, she didn't meet Genevieve's eyes.

Genevieve thought of everything she and Jeremy had shared over the years. Their past was so easy to picture, but she couldn't conjure up a picture of their future. "No, it wouldn't have." Genevieve's heart sped up at the sight of Harper's gray eyes. "We just weren't meant to be."

Harper pushed her plate away. "I don't know if I believe in such an idea."

"Why not?"

"Experience," Harper said with a sad smile. She clapped her hands against her stomach. "Well, I can't eat another bite, and I'm exhausted. Ready for the check?"

Genevieve nodded. Harper paid the bill quickly with the company credit card after a short protest from Genevieve and remained quiet until they stepped outside.

"Thank you for the company," Harper said.

"Thank you for the invite. I haven't eaten that well since I went home to see my mom last weekend." Genevieve was surprised when Harper gripped her elbow gently and started to walk her to where she was parked behind Harper's car. "Thank you again," Genevieve whispered.

Harper blinked slowly and looked into Genevieve's eyes for a moment. The gentle smile she wore never faltered.

"Good night, Genevieve. I'll see you in the morning." Harper turned away and walked to her car.

Genevieve drove home with her head lost in a thought tornado. She recalled the way Harper shut down when she'd asked her about her relationships or lack thereof. Someone had obviously hurt Harper in the past, but how could someone do such a thing? She thought of her own confession during dinner. Every word she spoke was true. What did that mean for her and Jeremy? Her life was spiraling away, and she needed to gain control of it fast.

STEP EIGHT

Expect the Unexpected

H ey, Gen!"

"What's up, Max?" She and Matthew were staring at her. She put down her pen to give them her full attention.

Maxine looked at Matthew and back to Genevieve. "Matthew is taking a poll for his next article. Do you think lesbians or gay men are more likely to fall for a good friend?"

Genevieve took off her glasses and started to clean them. She contemplated the question carefully, taking into account what she had learned about the gay community over the last couple of months. The answer seemed obvious. "Bisexuals," Genevieve said with confidence. "For sure."

Matthew rolled his eyes. "Well, duh. But bisexuals aren't included."

"Why not?" Genevieve said. "It's a valid sexuality. If bisexuals are the obvious choice here, I don't see why you're purposely excluding them."

Matthew's eyebrows rose slowly. "Is this a sensitive subject or…"

"No!" Her mind scrambled as if she just remembered her cover. "I just got into a debate the other day about the recognition of all sexualities." She had read an article instead of debating someone, but Matthew didn't need to know that.

"If I included every sexuality, my piece would turn from a short column to a sixteen page thesis," he said with a laugh, "so I narrowed it to the two." Matthew ran his fingers through his naturally platinum locks. "Now will you please answer the question?"

"It's tough to say because I think men are quick to act on attraction, but women are more emotional. If we're talking about falling for a friend, I'd have to say lesbians."

"Yes!" Maxine leaned forward with her hand outstretched for a high five. Genevieve was quick to give it to her. Matthew rolled his eyes. "Are you speaking from experience?" Maxine said to Genevieve.

Genevieve's eyes went wide. She had done so well dodging questions about her past. "Are you asking me if I've ever fallen for a friend?"

Maxine nodded earnestly. The older woman looked almost excited to hear an untold story. Genevieve didn't have the heart to deny her.

"Of course," she said, "haven't we all?" That earned an enthusiastic agreement from both of her coworkers.

"Who was it? Best friend? Teammate?" Maxine leaned forward.

Genevieve blurted out the first name that came to mind. "My best friend, Chloe. We were friends since grade school, and when it came time for college and becoming adults, we were there for each other's *curiosities.*"

Even Matthew seemed interested in Genevieve's story. "What happened?"

"After a few drunken nights together, I thought we had a deeper connection, but we didn't," Genevieve said wistfully. "She's still my best friend and always will be."

Clarissa approached their small group, apparently deciding to join the conversation. "Do you still love her?" she asked.

Genevieve cursed Clarissa's superhuman hearing. She needed to answer this question just the right way to keep Clarissa at bay with her intrusive comments and need to cause embarrassment. She put on her best solemn expression and said, "No, but I don't know if I'll ever be completely over her either."

"Good," Clarissa said, looking just beyond Genevieve. "Oh, hello, Harper."

Genevieve spun around quickly. "Harper!" She nearly squawked the name. "We were just helping Matthew with a poll about the deadly trap of falling for friends."

"Of course." Harper's unreadable expression fell away to a professional smile. "I hope it's turning out to be a good one." Harper pointed her attention to Matthew, who made his way back to his desk.

"One of my best pieces yet, naturally."

"And what are you working on, Clarissa?" Harper said in a tone that was all new to Genevieve, and she crossed her arms over her chest. Genevieve nearly shrank into herself.

"It's a secret right now, but I promise it'll turn you on."

Harper completely ignored Clarissa's now unnecessary presence. "I actually came by to talk to you, Genevieve." Everyone except Clarissa took that as their cue to get back to work. Harper cleared her throat. "How would you like to lend your advice to another review?"

Genevieve was surprised, to say the least. Harper wanted to spend time with her again so soon? "Sure," Genevieve said breathily. "What will it be this time?"

"Brunch. Are you free Saturday at noon?"

"I am." Even if she wasn't, Genevieve still would've answered yes.

"Great." Harper's face lit up, "I'll pick you up. It's street parking, so it makes more sense to take one car."

"Oh, okay," Genevieve stuttered, grabbing a notepad. "Let me give you my address."

Harper waved her off. "I already have it in your employee file."

Genevieve tilted her head and smirked. "Isn't that an abuse of power?"

"It's being resourceful." Harper looked at Genevieve, the soft smile never leaving her face. "I'll let you get back to work." Harper started to turn away but looked back briefly and nodded toward Genevieve's desk. "And your gummy bears." She left Genevieve in an excited stupor.

"Don't say I didn't try to warn you," Clarissa said as she sashayed away.

Genevieve fell back into her seat with a huff. "Whatever."

❖

Picking the perfect outfit for weekend brunch with a boss she'd been growing closer to as the days went by proved to be very difficult that Saturday morning. She didn't know the dress code for where they were going, but brunch wasn't really a black-tie affair. But she was also sure they weren't going to the beat-up diner down the street, so she couldn't be too casual.

Dress code aside, Genevieve wanted to look like she belonged with Harper, who always looked good. Genevieve froze, a pair of dark wash jeans in her hands. Did she want people to think she was *with* Harper? How would that make her feel? Genevieve's face flushed. Such an assumption would make her feel...wonderful. Harper was stunning, attentive, kind, and funny. If Genevieve was dating a woman, she'd be lucky for it to be Harper. A sly smile slid across Genevieve's face. *What the hell,* Genevieve thought, grabbing a burnt orange dress from her closet. *There's no shame in wanting to look good.*

A pair of navy blue tights and matching cardigan later, Genevieve was ready just as her doorbell rang. "Just a minute!" she called out as she slid on her heels. Her heartbeat picked up consistently with each step toward the door. Harper was early, but she seemed like the type who'd show up early everywhere she went. Genevieve couldn't hide either her surprise or disappointment when she found Jeremy waiting on the other side.

"Jeremy?"

"Gen!" He stepped forward and lifted Genevieve up into an enthusiastic hug. Genevieve landed on her feet gracelessly and pulled back to question her boyfriend, but he kissed her instead. "Hey, babe."

"Hey." Genevieve hurried him into her apartment and shut the door. "What are you doing here?"

"I came to surprise you!" He smiled goofily as he looked Genevieve up and down. "Did you know I was coming? Did Chloe tell you? I told her to keep it a secret."

"No, Chloe didn't tell me anything." Genevieve glanced at the clock. Harper would be there any minute.

"So you normally get this dressed up on Saturdays?" He sat down, taking up most of her couch.

"I have a work brunch to go to."

"Can you skip it? I came here so we could spend some time together. I didn't like how we left things the last time you came to visit." His puppy dog eyes shone, and Genevieve found herself able to resist them for the first time.

"I can't skip it, but you can hang out here." As if on cue, a knock sounded at the door. "That'll be my boss now."

"Your boss is picking you up?"

Genevieve ignored him. She was too busy trying to figure out the best way out of this situation. She took a deep breath and opened the door. Harper was standing in the hallway, all casual confidence with her hands in her pockets, smiling back at Genevieve. "Harper…"

"Hi," Harper said. "You look fantastic."

Genevieve fell into a shy stupor, tucking a strand of hair behind her ear and blushing. "Thank you." The moment ended as soon as Jeremy's deep voice bellowed from over her shoulder.

"Hey, I'm Jeremy." He stood up and extended his hand to Harper. "I'm Gen's—"

"Jeremy is one of my best friends from back home!" Genevieve answered enthusiastically through a tight smile. As casually as possible, she pushed her boyfriend back on the couch.

She leaned into Jeremy and whispered, "I'll explain everything when I get home."

"Jeremy is paying me a surprise visit," she said to Harper as she picked up her purse and moved toward the door.

"We can reschedule if you want." Harper's offer just added to the woman's undeniably considerate personality. Dammit if Genevieve didn't like her more for it.

"No," Genevieve said firmly. "I made plans with you, and I'm keeping them. I'd much rather go out with you." If any bit of honesty could come out of the situation she was currently in, this was it.

"Let's go then." Harper extended her bent elbow for Genevieve. "Shall we?" Genevieve felt a bit of herself melt at Harper's cute display of chivalry as she took her arm and they walked out into the autumn afternoon.

They spent the drive to the nearby restaurant in companionable silence. Genevieve was relieved Harper didn't ask any more questions about Jeremy, at least not before she had a chance to put together the answers. She tried to think of a story to tell, but her attention would always go back to Harper.

Harper's hands looked strong as they gripped the steering wheel, and her forearms flexed beneath the plush material of her sweater. Harper wore dark sunglasses that hid her eyes from Genevieve, but even those looked good on her. Harper's car was clean and sleek, much like its owner, and the interior smelled of new car and teakwood. Genevieve shook herself from the trance she was falling into.

Her boyfriend was back at her apartment, and his very presence was forgettable simply because Harper was next to her.

Then, in the bright sunlight of a November afternoon, Genevieve finally started to figure it out. She found Harper attractive. She didn't just appreciate the other woman aesthetically, she was attracted *to* her. When the realization hit her, she shifted her eyes away and turned toward the passenger side window.

"Genevieve," Harper said as she parked the car. "I have a confession to make." Genevieve turned to Harper so quickly her neck cramped. Her eyes were wide with fear. Harper couldn't possibly know what she was thinking, right? Harper lowered her sunglasses enough to look at her over the rim. "I invited you here under false pretenses."

"What? What's false about the pretenses?" She nearly smacked her own forehead for being so inarticulate.

"I've been here before, many times." Harper looked away and Genevieve was almost certain her boss was blushing. "I thought you might like it, and I enjoyed your company the other night. But when I came to ask you—"

"We had an audience."

"I didn't want any rumors going around all because of a friendly brunch."

Genevieve's heart sank in disappointment. "Yeah, of course."

Harper blew out a pent-up breath. "I'm glad I got that off my chest." Her million watt smile came to life. "Come on," Harper said and opened her car door. "I just know you're going to love this place."

Harper practically jumped from the car and went around to open Genevieve's door for her. In that split second alone, Genevieve scolded herself for being disappointed that Harper's interest in spending more time with her was purely platonic. She was the one with a boyfriend hiding in her apartment and a string of lies following her everywhere she went.

The second realization of her afternoon was harsh. She didn't even deserve Harper's friendship.

STEP NINE

Be Inquisitive and Patient

Genevieve settled into a safe silence during brunch. The lingering guilt from the car had followed her into the restaurant and wrapped around her heart in an icy grip. Instead of willingly participating in conversation, Genevieve focused on her food and thought of a way to resolve the entire situation with no one getting hurt. She folded her napkin and placed it on her lap before looking at Harper, who stared at her tenderly. *I don't want to hurt anyone but myself,* she thought resolutely.

"Tell me about Jeremy," Harper said. "Have you two been friends for long?" Harper sipped her coffee, seemingly oblivious to the way Genevieve was shifting anxiously.

"We, uh…grew up together." She gulped at her ice water. She wanted to tell Harper so much more, she *needed* to tell her the truth. "He's my boyfriend," she said in a small voice. She clamped her eyes shut and waited.

Harper didn't say a word.

Genevieve started to panic. Silence was worse than a torrent of words. She reopened her eyes to make sure Harper hadn't left. The other woman was still sitting across from her. She searched Harper's face for any sign of disgust or disappointment, but her expression gave nothing away.

"My boyfriend's name was Trevor," Harper said, "and we were together on and off through high school."

Confused, Genevieve shook her head. Harper had clearly misunderstood her. *This slip-up was a sign. Now isn't the time for me to explain. I'll have to wait for another opportunity,* Genevieve thought resolutely. She chose to keep the focus on Harper and opted to use humor as a deflection.

"Trevor and Harper?"

Harper laughed. "Like two characters out of a bad teen romance."

"Sounds like an accurate description." Genevieve took a slow sip from her water. "Tell me more."

"About Trevor?"

"About Harper." Genevieve pushed aside her empty plate and leaned forward on her elbows. Harper never broke eye contact as she mirrored Genevieve's actions and leaned forward. Harper's sweater hugged her defined upper arms enticingly, and Genevieve swallowed against a dry throat, this time not from anxiety or guilt.

"What would you like to know?" Harper's smile was encouraging, and Genevieve felt like this was her opportunity. If she wanted to know more about this brilliant, charming, gorgeous woman, now was the time to ask.

"Tell me about the young Harper Davies. Your family and your life growing up at the Jersey Shore." Genevieve settled back, getting comfortable for what she hoped would be a long story.

"Ah." Harper made a show of scratching her chin thoughtfully. "We're talking many years ago. I don't know if I can remember my younger days."

Genevieve rolled her eyes dramatically. "Ha ha, very funny. Now spill."

"Fine." Harper bit her lower lip, making Genevieve

wonder if she was nervous. "I didn't know my mother very well, and she didn't know my father at all. She was into some heavy-duty drugs by the time I was a toddler. Her brother, my uncle Will, tried to stage a few interventions, but they never worked. At least that's how he told the story." Genevieve picked up on the use of the past tense, and she prepared herself for a sad tale.

"Can I get you something else?" Their waiter stopped next to the table and started clearing their empty plates.

Harper was the first to answer. "No, thank—"

"Do you have pie?" Genevieve said abruptly. She might have been full, but she wasn't ready for her time with Harper to be over, not before she learned more about her. Harper looked at her with an amused smirk, and Genevieve shrugged. "I like pie."

"We have apple, coconut custard, and shoo fly pie."

Genevieve smiled brightly. "Apple, please."

"I guess I'll take another coffee, then."

"I'll be right back with that." The waiter nodded politely and left them.

Genevieve looked to Harper expectantly. "Please continue."

"After a while and countless visits from child services, my uncle gained full custody of me. It was for the best, not just because my mother was clearly unfit to be a parent, but because Uncle Will was gay. Growing up in this area and having him as an example, I never really saw the negative stigma that homosexuality had." Harper paused when the waiter brought two coffees and a slice of pie.

"Then why the boyfriend?"

"I knew what being gay *was,* but I didn't know what it felt like."

"And what does it feel like? For you, I mean," Genevieve

said, genuinely curious. She needed to know where those feelings came from and how someone just knew they fit. Genevieve waited patiently for the answer as she took her first bite of pie.

"It feels normal, comfortable. Like I'm not *trying* to be me, I just *am* me. Does that make sense?"

Genevieve tilted her head. She thought of all the ways she had changed since moving to New Jersey, how every day she went about her life the way she wanted to and did very little to try to fit the mold of what was expected of her. Crafty lies aside, she was more herself now than she had ever been in Pennsylvania.

Genevieve nodded enthusiastically. "It makes complete sense. That's how I've felt since I've moved here."

Harper flashed her a radiant smile. "I'm very happy to hear that."

"How did you find yourself in the boss's chair at *Out Shore*?"

"Will started the magazine when I was in my early twenties. He kept begging me to join the team, to help him get everything up and running, but I was fresh out of college and…" Harper paused as a blush crept along her cheeks. "I only managed minimal hours with Will because I was busy enjoying life."

"Enjoying life or enjoying women?"

Harper lowered her face and groaned. "I was enjoying my life *because* of the women." She looked up. "You have to remember, I was much younger, so I was in better shape then."

"Oh, I saw the pictures in your office." Genevieve finished off her pie and instantly regretted the overindulgence. If she were to take a deep breath, her dress would pop at the seams.

"So you agree?" Harper crossed her arms over her chest and sat back.

"If you're asking for my opinion, I'd say you've gotten better with age." Genevieve couldn't find one detail of Harper's appearance she'd deem as unattractive—not the hint of a silvery sparkle the sporadic grays leant to her dark hair or the way her few wrinkles framed her light eyes.

"Thank you," Harper said in a hushed whisper.

Their waiter appeared again, much to the surprise of both women. "Anything else?"

"Oh dear God, no!" Genevieve held her stomach.

"Just the check, thank you." Harper laughed and chastised her gently. "You *had* to have pie."

"I regret nothing." Genevieve said, exhaling heavily. "When did your uncle put you in charge?"

"He died when I was twenty eight."

"I'm sorry." Genevieve reached out and took Harper's hand. She traced her thumb over the surprisingly soft skin, feeling the sensation throughout her entire body.

"Thank you." Harper gripped Genevieve's hand tightly for a moment before releasing it. Genevieve missed the contact immediately but pushed her disappointment aside.

"And here you are—Harper Davies, woman in charge."

Harper laughed. "Yes, after much trial and error, here I am."

"You're doing great, Harper. Will would be very proud of you."

Harper stared at Genevieve for quiet moments. Her throat flexed a few times and she chewed at the inside of her cheek. If Genevieve had to guess, Harper was fighting a swell of emotion.

Instead of focusing on Harper's vulnerability, Genevieve changed the subject. "I think it's time to get me out of here before I explode." She reached for her purse, but Harper waved her off immediately.

"I got it." Harper took out a personal credit card, a detail Genevieve noticed right away. "I'm the one keeping you from an old friend."

"Sometimes our new friends are more important." They looked at one another, an unexpected tension crackling between them.

Harper cleared her throat roughly. "Let's get you back to Jeremy."

"Yeah." During their meal she had completely forgotten about her boyfriend who was sitting, clueless, back at her apartment. "Jeremy."

❖

Jeremy was off the couch the moment Genevieve stepped through the door. "What the hell was that all about?"

She stared at him quizzically. "Were you just sitting there this whole time?"

"No. I went to the bathroom and ate the leftover pizza that was in the fridge."

Genevieve grimaced. That pizza was a week old.

"But whatever, that doesn't matter. You need to tell me what's going on."

Genevieve sighed and dropped onto the couch. "That was my boss."

"I got that much."

"She runs *Out Shore Magazine*." Genevieve ran her fingers through her straight hair roughly.

"Yes, bosses run things. You're supposed to be telling me things I don't know, Gen."

"And maybe if you didn't have a smart-ass comment for everything I said, I'd get to my point more quickly." Genevieve had always hated the way Jeremy employed sarcasm to escalate an argument that wasn't even started.

"Fine." He sat beside her and crossed his arms.

"*Out Shore Magazine* is one of the top LGBT publications on the East Coast. Having any writing experience with them will look amazing on a resume…" Genevieve let her statement trail off, hoping Jeremy would be quick enough to put two and two together. The way he was just staring at her killed those hopes. "LGBT—you know how you always say I go into things with blinders on and end up in crazy situations?"

"Yeah, all the time." He looked at her in confusion at first, but his eyes went wide. "Gen, no."

"Gen, yes."

"So they think you're gay?"

"They think I'm gay and *single*. That's sort of what my column is about—being a new lesbian in town, trying to make a life for myself." She wiped her face and looked at him. His face was blank.

"You've got to be kidding me!" Jeremy's voice was too loud for Genevieve's small apartment. "How does that even work? Do you not talk about life before New Jersey?"

Genevieve pressed her fingertips to her temples. "I'm careful about what I say and make sure to modify some of the details."

"Modify some details? Gen, do you hear yourself?"

"Well, so far I've been pretty successful. My column is one of the most popular, and I've been making some friends at work—"

"By lying to them!" Jeremy started laughing. "This has to be the most idiotic thing you've ever done. And that's saying something."

"Excuse me?" Genevieve sat back from Jeremy enough

to see the amused look on his face. "What the hell is that supposed to mean?"

Jeremy froze mid-laugh, and his smile faltered. "Don't take it like that."

"Like what? Like my boyfriend just called me an idiot?" Genevieve stormed off to her bedroom, changing out of her dress and into pajamas. The day was still early, but she was ready for it to be done.

"Gen, come on." Jeremy leaned against the doorway, and Genevieve cursed the fact that she didn't shut the door.

"You really should've called," Genevieve said as she put her hair up haphazardly.

"That wouldn't have been much of a surprise then."

"Your surprise isn't working out very well anyway." Genevieve walked past him, not stopping until she had an ice-cold beer in her hand. After one large sip, Genevieve said, "If you leave now, it won't be dark for much of the drive."

"Wait…what?" Jeremy's mouth hung open.

Genevieve squared her shoulders. "I think you should go."

"Don't be ridiculous."

"I guess I'm just a ridiculous idiot!" Genevieve slammed her beer down on her kitchen counter.

"Gen, listen to yourself." Jeremy gripped Genevieve by her elbows. He looked at her earnestly as he continued. "I drove all the way here to see my girlfriend, to *surprise* my girlfriend, then she lays all this craziness on me, and now she's going to kick me out because I didn't react exactly as she hoped."

Genevieve blinked at him. He wasn't exactly wrong, and that annoyed her even more. "You called your girlfriend an idiot."

"No I didn't." Jeremy shook his head. "That's how you took it."

Genevieve took a deep breath. She could continue this

argumentative loop or surrender and go on with her day only somewhat agitated. If history had taught her anything, it was to just let this go or Jeremy would be unbearable.

Unsurprisingly, he smiled in victory. "That's my girl." He wrapped his bulky arms around Genevieve. She felt suffocated by the embrace and by his presence.

"You may have wanted to surprise me, but it really would've been best if you had called. I have some work to get done." Genevieve stepped away and walked to take a seat at her desk.

"Forget about work!" Jeremy waved his hands. "I'm here! Let's either go out or go to the bedroom." His wide smile was infectious. Genevieve felt herself surrendering for the second time already.

"Let me write for an hour, and then we can do whatever you want." Genevieve opened her laptop and hoped an hour would be enough time to muster up some excitement for Jeremy's visit.

STEP TEN

Be Prepared for When Things Don't Go as Planned

The incessant ringing of her cell phone awoke Genevieve harshly the following Saturday morning. She had an uneventful week, free from Harper's comforting and confusing presence thanks to Harper's week-long business trip to the West Coast. Genevieve rolled over and opened one eye. The display of her phone was out of focus but she answered anyway.

"H'llo?" Genevieve maneuvered into a comfortable position and pulled the covers over her head.

"Genevieve?"

Genevieve shuffled through all the familiar voices in her memory, but this one was new. "Yeah?" Her voice crackled with sleep.

"It's Harper. I'm sorry it's so early."

Genevieve sat straight up in bed. "What happened? What is it?" She was already standing and pulling pants from her dresser.

"Nothing happened," Harper said. "I have a huge favor to ask of you."

Genevieve fell back onto her bed and breathed deeply. The fog left her head as her heartbeat started to slow down. "Of course, anything you need."

"My flight from California gets in at five o'clock your

time, and my ride home just bailed on me. I tried a few other people, but no one could make it."

"I'll pick you up, don't worry about it."

"Great. That's a relief. A cab fare from Newark would be brutal."

"No worries, it'll give me a good excuse to explore outside of Asbury."

Harper chuckled. "You won't see much on your drive to the airport, but I'll try my best to keep you entertained on the way back." Genevieve warmed at the idea. "Genevieve?"

"Yeah?"

"Did I wake you?"

Genevieve blushed. "You may have."

"It's after eleven there."

"I like my sleep."

"Beauty sleep, I get it." Genevieve's blush intensified. Silence stretched on before a muffled, robotic voice sounded in the background. "My flight is boarding. I'll text you the details so you know where to get me."

"Sounds good."

"I'll see you soon. Thanks again, Genevieve. You're a lifesaver." Harper hung up.

Genevieve's face split into a wide grin. She hurried into the bathroom, needing a shower before spending time in a car with Harper. The ride to the airport would take a while, Genevieve was sure of that. She paused. She had no idea where the airport was. The shower would have to wait until she did a little research.

She spent the early afternoon finding the perfect directions to Newark airport, printing them out, making notes in the margins of the paper, and plugging the information into two separate map applications she had on her phone. She ate a small lunch and managed a quick shower.

Genevieve's 1997 Toyota had treated her well through the years and it had cost her very little to maintain. The car was so well kept, no one would suspect it was as old as it actually was. *Maybe after my first year with the magazine I'll treat myself to something newer,* Genevieve mused as she settled behind the wheel. She turned the key and checked to make sure the heat was on. The last thing she wanted was for Harper to arrive from sunny California and climb into a freezer on wheels. She was so desperate for Harper to enjoy the ride, she even created a special playlist of classic driving music and modern hits.

"Shit!" Genevieve slapped the steering wheel. She had forgotten her iPod in her apartment. She still had time to run back.

Genevieve grabbed her purse, got out of her car, and ran to her apartment, taking the stairs two at time. When she got to her door, she dug through her purse for her key. Her head fell back when she realized she had left her keys in the ignition. Genevieve grumbled to herself as she ran back to the car. The door wouldn't budge. She tried again, pulling at the handle desperately.

"No, no, no…" Genevieve peered into the window and saw her Care Bear keychain dangling from the steering column. Genevieve stomped at the ground and cursed under breath.

Jeremy had her spare set of keys, and she didn't want to break the window. All she could think of was to call Maxine or Matthew and ask if she could borrow their car. Thankfully, her phone was still in her purse as were her printed directions to the airport.

Matthew didn't answer the phone, but Maxine picked up on the second ring. "Maxine!"

"Gen?"

"Yeah, it's me. Listen I need a big favor. Are you home?"

"I am…" Genevieve could hear the skepticism in Maxine's voice.

"I locked my keys in my car, and I promised Harper I'd pick her up at the airport in an hour and nine minutes. Would you be able to come by, let me borrow your car, and wait for roadside assistance to get here?" Genevieve grimaced at the list of favors. "Lunch will be on me all week," she offered.

"Gen, as much as I'd like to help you, Connie has the car right now."

"Shit." Time was ticking away. How was Genevieve going to explain this to Harper? "Okay, thanks anyway."

"Wait, I think I have another idea. My neighbor is an older guy who barely goes anywhere, and I've been mowing his lawn for years. The guy owes me. Give me your address and fifteen minutes. I'll be there."

Genevieve relayed all the necessary information and promised not just lunch for the week, but drinks as well.

Twenty-two minutes later, Maxine showed up in a nondescript minivan from the eighties. Genevieve fired off a text to Harper letting her know she was running a little late, but she was on her way. The hypnotic sway of the fuzzy dice hanging from the rearview mirror did not calm her anxiety. She stuck to the slow lane all the way up the Garden State Parkway, afraid the van wouldn't handle more than sixty-five miles per hour.

She pulled into the pickup line at Newark airport forty minutes later than planned, and she spotted Harper sitting on her suitcase not too far from the doors. Genevieve honked, and Harper looked up from her phone for a moment before spotting her. Harper smiled brightly, and she tilted her head when she took in the rest of her ride.

Harper stowed her suitcase away in the back and took her place in the passenger seat. "Hi, thanks again for the ride."

"This isn't mine," Genevieve said before Harper had the chance to ask. "Mine isn't much better, but it's not a minivan." Harper smiled at her softly. Genevieve wondered how someone could manage to look so good after over five hours on an airplane. Harper's hair was perfectly styled, her gray eyes bright and clear, and her khakis and navy blue sweatshirt were barely creased.

A car horn blared behind Genevieve, and she hastily stepped on the gas. The van bucked into motion. She looked at Harper sheepishly. "Sorry."

"It's fine. If you don't mind me asking, if this isn't yours..."

"I could tell you the whole long story, or you could take my word for it that today is just another day in the life of Genevieve Applegate." Genevieve shot Harper her most charming smile.

"Long stories and long car rides go hand in hand."

Genevieve told Harper about her detailed preparations for the drive to northern Jersey and how she was supposed to arrive with nearly twenty minutes to spare. Harper fell into a fit of laughter and tears when Genevieve finally told her that it all fell apart and how she owed Maxine, big time.

"This is the usual for you?" Harper wiped away an errant laughter-caused tear.

"Pretty much." Genevieve shrugged and changed lanes. "I used to say if it wasn't for bad luck, I'd have none at all, but I've come to realize it's not bad luck. I just have my own special brand."

They fell silent as Genevieve maneuvered about the parkway. Trees passed the window in blurry streaks. Harper had switched on the radio to a popular station, and they sang and bopped along to their favorite songs. By the time they'd reached their exit, they were all smiles.

"Just make like you're heading to work. I don't live very far from the office. Any big plans for Thanksgiving?" Harper said.

"Going home to have dinner with my family. What about you?"

"Nothing, really, just a quiet day at home with the parade and the dog show."

"No company?"

"No company."

Genevieve wanted to ask more, but she also wanted to be respectful of Harper's privacy. Even though Harper seemed content with her holiday plans, that wasn't enough for Genevieve.

"Do you prefer it that way?" She hoped the sad image she had of Harper sitting at dinner table alone was inaccurate.

"It's better than conversations with distant relatives or awkwardly trying to fit in at a friend's dinner party." Genevieve wasn't sure if Harper's smile was forced or not. "I get to stay in my pajamas all day and eat whatever I want in whatever order I want. It's not so bad. I even start with dessert for breakfast," Harper said with a lopsided grin.

Genevieve nodded, unsure of what to say. She kept looking between the road and Harper with an uneasiness settling in her chest. Her lips were in a tight pout for the remainder of the drive. As she pulled up to Harper's home, she wasn't surprised to see that Harper had a nice house, but she hadn't expected such immaculate and expansive landscaping. "Wow…"

"What?" Harper looked bemused.

"I bet this is beautiful in the summer." Genevieve looked at the variety of trees, shrubbery, and slightly shriveled plants.

She could picture just how colorful it'd appear on a sunny June day. She could easily get lost in the fantasy of sitting on the covered front porch, drinking a tea and reading a worn paperback.

"It is." She climbed out of the van and pulled her suitcase out of the back. "Thanks again, Genevieve," Harper said. "I owe you one."

"You owe me nothing." Genevieve shook her head. "I was happy to help."

"If it makes you feel any better, you make the van look good," Harper said with a wink. "See you Monday."

Genevieve said a coy good-bye and watched until Harper entered her house safely. She finally released a long breath and turned back toward the highway. She replayed Harper's wink over and over again as she drove. If she didn't know any better, she'd think Harper was flirting with her.

STEP ELEVEN

Be Open to New Experiences

Genevieve saw the word *organic* everywhere she looked. She couldn't navigate the produce section or the fresh meats without seeing those seven letters plastered across every display. Was the difference really worth the extra forty-seven cents a pound? Maybe it was time for her to explore more food options than pricey takeout and cold cereal. This was the first time Genevieve had gone food shopping since moving to Asbury, and she was loath to admit that she wasn't doing it for herself. Food shopping was much more pleasant when you were doing it for someone else.

She scanned the area where several signs for fresh turkey were lined up, but she didn't see one package of poultry. Genevieve looked around for a staff member to help her.

"Excuse me?" she called out to a middle-aged man behind the butcher counter. Judging by the multitude of stains on his long white coat and his disgruntled look, he'd had a busy day. "Do you have any fresh turkey breast left?"

"The day before Thanksgiving?" he scoffed. "We put out the last of it about an hour ago. Good luck." He disappeared behind large swinging doors.

She mumbled under her breath. "Thanks."

"And here I thought I was the only last-minute shopper

in this store," said a gentle voice behind Genevieve. She turned to see an attractive brunette eyeing her cart, half-filled with Thanksgiving essentials. Genevieve looked at the other woman's cart, and the first thing she noticed was a fresh turkey.

"Looks like your last minute shopping was much more successful than mine."

"I know a place. Follow me." She tilted her head to the side and walked away. Genevieve stood still for a moment before following this stranger who was a member of some elite poultry club.

After weaving in and out of the small groups of people crowding the store's aisles, they came to stop at the end of a refrigerated section. The sign on the endcap boasted Fresh Farm-Raised Organic Turkey. Genevieve hesitated momentarily when she saw the price was seventy-five cents more a pound, but her desperation for turkey outweighed her light wallet.

"Pricey, I know, but this is the only place in the area that has anything fresh."

"No, it's great, thank you." She finally took a moment to look at her fellow shopper turned savior. The stranger was very attractive. Her makeup was impeccable, and warm, cozy clothing hugged every curve. She had the kind of long, thick hair that bounced with an effortless wave.

The woman smiled shyly. "What brings you to the market so last minute? I just found out my mother had a fight with my aunt and wants to have Thanksgiving with just us." She rolled her eyes. "I'm ecstatic, can't you tell?" Genevieve couldn't help but laugh.

Genevieve hesitated. She was talking to a complete stranger, so surely she could be a little more honest about her intentions and situation. "Someone I care for very deeply was planning on spending Thanksgiving alone." Genevieve pushed wisps of hair from her face. "That didn't sit very well with me."

"That's awfully kind of you." She leaned forward a bit.

"I'm Gen." She put out her hand. "And you are?"

"Melanie." They shook hands briefly and shared a friendly smile. "This is going to sound a little forward, but I've got a fresh bird in my cart and need to start preparations soon. So, this person you care for...boyfriend or girlfriend?"

"She's not my girlfriend." Genevieve mulled the answer over and in a split second swell of bravery, said, "But I think about what could be."

"Ah." Melanie snapped her fingers. "I was going to ask for your number."

Genevieve was shocked. That surprise must've been broadcast across her face because Melanie started to laugh and bowed her head, effectively hiding her blush. "W-why?"

"Because." Melanie slid her hands into the back pockets of her snug jeans. Genevieve was afraid she wouldn't elaborate, but she did. "You're cute, like *really* cute, and kind. I would've bit that butcher's head off if he had talked to me like that." She giggled lightly.

"Thank you, I'm flattered but..."

"I know, I know. I'll tell you what, Gen. I'm going to give you my number anyway." She pulled a pen and slip of paper from her purse and started to scribble away. "Because you're not taken yet." She winked and said good-bye before heading toward the registers.

Genevieve stood still in a sea of shoppers, one hand resting on her cart and the other gripping tightly to a scrap of paper. *Did she just...?* Genevieve thought. She looked at the phone number in her hand and smiled. For the first time, someone had paid that kind of attention to her, aside from the same men who'd hoot and whistle at her every time she'd walk by or into the local bar in Milan. She'd never really been hit on before. Genevieve considered her admirer. *Yes, she's definitely attractive*, she thought with a smirk.

She made her way through the rest of her shopping list with a skip to her step.

❖

"Hey, guys!" Genevieve greeted her coworkers brightly and loudly enough to be heard over the robust chatter that filled the small pub.

"Look who finally decided to take us up on our invitation!" Matthew stood and hugged Genevieve.

Maxine pushed Matthew out of the way and enveloped Genevieve in a robust hug. "How are you, kid?"

"I'm doing well." Genevieve removed her coat and sat at the cozy round table. Maxine and Matthew were the only two of the six coworkers she really knew at the table, but she recognized the others as designers from the graphics department. She was thankful that one particular coworker was absent. "No Clarissa?"

"Wish she was here?" Maxine said.

"Yes, I'm devastated."

"Actually, she doesn't come out with us very often. I can't even remember the last time," Matthew said, sitting back in his chair.

"Really? You two seem so close at work. I was convinced you were each other's wingman, or wingwoman, whatever you'd call it."

Matthew snorted. "Hardly. We share stories, sure, but Clarissa is pretty private, believe it or not."

"What about you?" Genevieve said, turning in her chair to face Maxine.

Maxine popped a pretzel in her mouth and chewed slowly. "I've known Clarissa for a long time now, and I'd agree with Matthew. She's private, and a lot of what you see at work is for show. Her role as the head of Sex and Relationships is just that—a role."

"A role she fills *very* well," Matthew said, leaning forward. "Do you have any idea how many pairs of panties have been mailed to the office?"

Genevieve grew uncomfortable with how closely this conversation resembled gossip, so she filed this information away and turned her full attention back to their celebrations.

"So, you guys do this every year?"

"Every year," a middle-aged blonde said. "I'm Pauline, by the way." She extended her hand. Genevieve took it quickly, surprised by a firm grip. "This is Ron and Steve." She nodded to the two men beside her.

"Nice to meet you all," Genevieve said meekly.

"We started this a few years ago, when we were all reminiscing about our wild college days and how the night before Thanksgiving was *the* night to go out."

"Why was this night so special? Thank you." Genevieve smiled at Matthew as he set a cold pint of beer down in front of her.

"Did you go away to college?" Pauline said.

"No."

"That explains it. The Wednesday before Thanksgiving is the day everyone comes home from school, so it's like a reunion every year." Pauline popped a few complimentary peanuts in her mouth and chewed. "We're not in college anymore, but that doesn't mean we can't have fun."

"Where did you go to school, Gen?" Maxine's question

was innocent, but Genevieve had been very vague when it came to any talk of her past.

Genevieve bought herself an extra moment by sipping her beer. "A small community college by me."

"Lots of good ol' boys chasing your skirt, I'm sure." Matthew nudged her with his elbow.

"Not really." With Jeremy by her side, not one guy would be willing to risk a confrontation by talking to her.

"What about women?" Pauline said.

"Oh, God no. I lived in a very straightlaced area, in every sense."

Pauline shuddered, and the table erupted with laughter.

"Living here must be a nice change, then," Steve said.

Genevieve nodded. "Very nice." She debated whether to tell them about her run-in at the store earlier, but she wasn't sure the story would be as juicy to them.

Maxine caught not just her smile, but she must've also noticed Genevieve's conflict. "What's that look about?" Maxine said, sliding her chair closer to Genevieve.

Genevieve kept her eyes down and tried to hide her growing smile. "Nothing really."

"Okay, seriously," Matthew said, holding up his hand. "Spill."

Genevieve took a deep breath. "I sort of got hit on at the grocery store today." She sat back and crossed her arms over her chest, feigning a nonchalant attitude. Meanwhile, her insides were shaking with anticipation for the group's reaction. Surprisingly, Steve was the first to acknowledge her.

"Oh," he said with a sigh. "I love random moments like that. They're so romantic."

"The romance factor depends on the aisle they were in," Matthew said, earning an eye roll from Maxine. "What?

Like you could find an iota of romance in being hit on while standing in front of a wall of raw meat!"

"Turkeys," Genevieve said.

"What?" several people from around the table asked at once.

"We were standing in front of turkeys, and she gave me her number." Genevieve took a long sip of her beer. "That was after she told me I was 'really cute.'" She smiled broadly at the not-so-distant memory.

Matthew brushed away the comment with a hand flourish. "We know *you're* cute, but what did *she* look like?"

"Beautiful. Long hair so brown, it was nearly black. A few inches taller than me and curvy, with gorgeous green eyes and the most adorable freckles." Genevieve's smile faltered slightly when she realized nothing she said felt odd or unnatural. She wasn't faking any of this.

"Are you going to call her?" Pauline said, her voice piercing the heavy silence that engulfed their table.

Genevieve swallowed roughly. "I don't think so. She's not really my type."

"She sounds like my type," Pauline said.

"What *is* your type?" Matthew said.

Harper immediately popped into her mind. "I prefer less feminine women."

"So you like butch women," Maxine said proudly.

Genevieve tried to apply the word to Harper, and it just didn't fit. "Not necessarily," she said gently, careful not to offend Maxine. "A little more on the masculine side, but a bit softer." She flicked a peanut into her mouth.

"Like Harper!" Ron said, and Genevieve choked.

Both Matthew and Maxine started patting her on the back. She could breathe, but she couldn't shake the tickle causing her to choke, which also made her unable to speak. No amount of hand waving or head shaking would make them stop pounding her back. Finally, she pushed away from the table.

"I'm okay!" Genevieve took a deep breath. She coughed a few more times and cleared her throat roughly.

"A lesbian choking on nuts," Matthew said. "That's not something you see every day."

Step Twelve

Show Off Your Talents

Yes, Mom," Genevieve said for the fifth time. "I know, everyone will be there and Grandma was expecting me." Genevieve rolled her eyes before double-checking the seal on one of the many Tupperware containers on her passenger seat.

"I still don't understand why you'd choose not to be with your family on Thanksgiving."

"Mom, I'm not choosing *against* my family, I'm just choosing to be a good friend."

"Is this because of the fight you had with Jeremy?"

Genevieve nearly slammed on the brakes as she approached a red light. "He told you about that?"

"He didn't go into detail, but he told me his visit was a bit rocky at first. I just don't want something like that to keep you from coming home."

Genevieve sighed. "I told you, I'm just being a good friend."

"You could've brought your friend here!"

At this, Genevieve laughed heartily. "No, Mom, I couldn't, but I know you would've fed her if I did. Listen, I have to go," she said as she parked her car. "I love you and happy

Thanksgiving." Genevieve ended the phone call and looked out her car window.

She wasn't entirely sure why she had come to this decision. She shook her head and laughed at herself. She knew exactly why she had. Genevieve was a victim of the sad look of resignation that shone in Harper's dreamy gray eyes when she talked about spending the holiday alone. Harper had even sounded sullen as she wished everyone at the office a happy Thanksgiving.

Harper showed unwavering generosity toward the people in her life, and Genevieve felt she deserved the same in return. She couldn't leave Harper to celebrate alone. Now she just hoped surprising Harper wasn't a terrible idea.

Genevieve gathered all of her containers, saying a silent prayer of thanks that her mother had taught her how to prepare the annual meal, and went up Harper's front walk. Genevieve grew more apprehensive with each step. What if Harper had invited someone over already? What if she preferred spending Thanksgiving alone? Genevieve stood frozen in place, staring at Harper's front door. She saw a shadow passing by the window, so she knocked tentatively.

As Harper opened the door, a comically puzzled look overtook her face. "Genevieve?"

"Harper." Genevieve was nearly breathless from nerves, straining to hold on to the stacked containers. She had prepared an entire meal, packed it up, and driven the short distance to Harper's home, but never once considered what she'd say once she arrived. "I forgot wine."

Harper looked at Genevieve and smiled. "Of course you did. You don't like wine, but I'm more curious about what you remembered."

"I have everything else covered, I mean, just in case you

wanted some company and a home-cooked Thanksgiving dinner?" Genevieve shifted from side to side. She waited patiently for Harper's verdict, but the meal in her hands grew heavier with each passing moment.

"You know I'm a fan of good company."

"What about the food?"

"Just an added bonus, I guess." They looked into one another's eyes, and Genevieve's chest tightened pleasurably. "Come in." Harper stepped to the side.

Harper's home had an open layout. She'd decorated in clean, neutral colors that kept the space light. It felt distinctly like Harper. "I hope you weren't cooking. Where should I put these?"

"Head straight back to the kitchen, and don't worry. I was planning on a sandwich and ice cream." Harper pointed Genevieve in the right direction. "Just give me a minute to change." She signaled down to her gray sweatpants and navy blue T-shirt.

"Don't," Genevieve said a little too forcefully. She blushed. "This is your home. Stay comfortable." Harper had no reason to change for a day spent at home, and Genevieve wanted to indulge in this version of Harper. Her boss's hair was even without product, a few dark locks falling upon her forehead.

Harper smirked. "I'll get the plates, then."

They worked together in the kitchen, filling two plates with a sinful amount of food. Genevieve watched Harper out of the corner of her eye the whole time and soaked up the domestic feeling that enveloped her. She could blame the holiday or even Harper's warm and welcoming personality, but Genevieve was overwhelmed with glee and comfort.

"What about your family?" Harper said.

"What about them?"

"I thought you were spending the day back in Pennsylvania."

Genevieve shrugged. "That was the original plan, but I didn't like the idea of you being alone."

"Why? I'm used to being alone."

"No one should be alone on Thanksgiving." *Especially not you,* she thought.

"Thank you." Harper's face was blank, but her eyes were stormy with emotion. Genevieve knew she'd done the right thing. "And the good news is I have wine and craft beer."

They ate a lot, and talked easily and openly, much like they usually did when they shared a meal. But Harper looked more comfortable at home. Genevieve apologized again as she cleaned the last bits of cranberry sauce from her plate.

"I really should've called first."

"Genevieve, don't apologize. This was a wonderful surprise." Harper looked over her shoulder at the pumpkin pie. "I love edible surprises."

Genevieve sat back in her seat, a smile of satisfaction lighting up her face, and looked at Harper, whose eyes were big with excitement as she eyed their dessert. *She's dreamy,* Genevieve thought. Harper was so naturally beautiful, Genevieve caught herself wanting to tell her boss as much. She cleared her throat instead and stood to clear the table.

"Don't you dare." Harper reached out and gripped Genevieve's wrist gently, her thumb tracing the delicate skin there for a moment. "Grab another beer and head to the couch. I'll clean up quickly and meet you there with dessert."

Genevieve did as she was told, sitting in Harper's living room with a fresh beer and waiting for her host to join her. A flat-screen television hung on the wall above a modern glass fireplace. The sofa was a large, L-shaped piece in a light gray that accented the dark hardwood floors and white area rugs. Genevieve's favorite part of the room was the orange throw pillows, the pop of color cheering the space up. The built-in bookcases that lined the wall were bursting with both hard- and soft-cover volumes, picture frames on the few empty shelves. Harper's smiling face was in most, but they were all centered around a stunning portrait of her uncle. Genevieve's heart ached when she thought of Harper dealing with such a loss.

"I should have offered you coffee or tea," Harper called out from the kitchen. "Now it looks like I'm trying to liquor you up."

"I already knew you were." Genevieve took another sip of her lager. "I'm really okay with beer." She settled back into the sofa after setting her drink on a glass coffee table, the plush cushions embracing her.

"You look comfortable," Harper said from the edge of the room.

Genevieve placed her hand on the cushion beside her and ran her fingertips along the soft cloth. Her eyes were slightly hooded and the smile she shot Harper was pure ecstasy. "You bought this couch to seduce women," she said. Harper blushed and stuttered. As cute as the sight was, Genevieve saved her. "Join me," she said, patting the couch.

Harper sat and Genevieve didn't do much to fight off gravity as she slid into Harper's body. The contact was innocent, but intimate. Genevieve concentrated on the buzz traveling through her veins, up her arms, and settling in her chest.

"This has been one of the best Thanksgivings I've had," Harper whispered. Her eyes were closed, and Genevieve took the opportunity to observe the lines on her boss's slightly tanned face, a few faint freckles on the bridge of her nose.

Harper's lips were slightly parted and Genevieve wondered if they were as addicting when they were kissing as they were when they were smiling.

"What about you?" Harper said. She opened her eyes and looked at Genevieve. "I hope you're not regretting your decision."

"I'm definitely not." Harper's steely eyes were fixed on her mouth as well. Genevieve pulled back, putting space between them. She cleared her throat awkwardly. "So, uh, what do you usually watch now?"

"I usually put on whatever Christmas classic they're airing prematurely." Harper reached for the remote, clearly unshaken by the moment. Genevieve wondered if she had imagined it.

"Sounds perfect." Genevieve burrowed deeper into the pillows, hoping her drowsiness would help calm her shaky nerves. God, she wanted to kiss Harper so badly, and when she saw Harper felt the same, she panicked.

Her career plan was unfolding wrong. She wasn't supposed to end up in a budding romance with her female boss while posing as a lesbian. Every lie was so easy to forget with each passing day. Genevieve's life in Asbury felt more like her truth the more she lived it. But an attraction? An honest-to-God attraction to someone's mind, body, and soul? An attraction to everything about them? This was not in Genevieve's plan.

"Do you want to stay here tonight?"

"What?" Genevieve sat straight up, startled by Harper's question.

"You can spend the night if you're getting tired." Harper's eyes started to widen as realization dawned. "I have a guest bedroom and bathroom," she said. "I even have some clothes you can borrow."

Genevieve weighed her options. The temptation to stay was great. She was sleepy, for sure, but would she be able to keep herself in check while spending a night under the same roof as Harper? No. For once, Genevieve was going to think things through before acting. Harper would not be another brash decision, another ridiculous story to add to Genevieve's repertoire. Harper mattered, and that fact made Genevieve feel sick.

"Are you okay? Genevieve?" Harper reached over and placed her hand between Genevieve's shoulder blades.

"I'm fine." Genevieve stood a little too quickly. Her head spun slightly. "I think I'll get going."

"Can you drive?"

Genevieve's heart was swelling and breaking all at once as she sank into the soft kindness in Harper's eyes. "I'm good to drive, I promise."

"If you say so." Harper walked Genevieve to the door, pausing briefly before pulling Genevieve into a hug. Genevieve breathed in deeply, relishing Harper's clean scent. "Text me when you get home so I know you're okay," she said directly into Genevieve's ear.

"I will." Genevieve released Harper slowly, reluctantly, before she opened the front door and stepped onto the stoop. Harper called her back suddenly.

"Thank you, for everything today. I really meant what I said." Harper didn't need to repeat herself. Genevieve knew exactly what she was referring to.

"I can't remember the last time I enjoyed Thanksgiving this much," Genevieve said. She stepped forward and hugged Harper again, this time leaving a small kiss on her cheek. Genevieve pulled back slightly. "You're welcome, and thank you for your hospitality. Good night, Harper."

"Good night, Genevieve."

The distance between them was minimal, and every crackling feeling Genevieve thought she'd imagined before was surely a reality. She lowered her head before walking to her car. She buckled herself in and started the car, Harper still standing in her open doorway, watching her as she left. Genevieve gave a tentative wave before pulling away from the curb. The moment she was gone, Genevieve started to cry.

STEP THIRTEEN

Don't Let Anything Get in Your Way

Genevieve spent the next lackluster weeks just going through the motions. She was in a near-emotionless daze. With so many warring emotions swirling around inside, she eventually shut down and decided to focus on work for the time being. Thankfully everyone became nearly robotic as the holidays approached, so Genevieve's odd behavior went unnoticed.

Out Shore was abuzz as Christmas approached. Their annual year-end double issue was going into print, which led to a full week off to celebrate the holidays accordingly. Genevieve was dreading this time off, but she told herself it'd be a good time to concentrate on a new project or one of the many things she had put on the back burner. Genevieve planned to work on anything else but herself.

"Hey, Gen!" Matthew startled her while she was making coffee. She looked at him with annoyance. "Who are you going to bring to the party?"

Genevieve looked around, realizing she was in the middle of an office powwow. She was tired and irritated by the inclusion, but she didn't want to be rude. "What party are we talking about?" She plastered on a stiff smile.

"The annual Christmas party," Clarissa purred from

behind her. "Everyone's invitation is a plus one." She looked at her manicure and said, "Even if you don't have anyone."

If only she was a snake like Clarissa, she'd be able to spit venom.

"It's a great time," Maxine said. She always seemed to speak right after Clarissa, as if she had to soothe Clarissa's words. "Every year tops the year before, even when we think it's impossible."

"I met two soul mates last year," Matthew said with a wistful smile. "I'm hoping for three this year."

"If you're hoping to meet three soul mates, who are you bringing as your plus one?" Genevieve said. She had stopped stirring her coffee and committed her full attention to the conversation.

"I go stag."

"I have a few possibilities," Clarissa said with an exaggerated flip of her red hair. "I just have to decide which one won't bore me after a few hours."

Genevieve ignored Clarissa. "Where is the party held?" she asked.

"Harper has it at her house every year," Maxine said. "Keeps the cost down, the location convenient, and the partygoers safer."

"Hmm." Genevieve pictured Harper's house full of guests and knew exactly how well it'd work out. She removed the spoon from her coffee. "She has enough space for it."

Clarissa backed her chair away from the table with a scrape and stormed off, knocking the spoon out of Genevieve's hand. It bounced to the floor and came to a stop just beside the break table. "Okay, seriously, what is her problem?" Genevieve snapped as she bent down to pick up her spoon. "Every time I talk or say something about Harper, she's a total b—"

She smacked her face into the edge of the plastic chair

Clarissa had vacated, stumbling back with her hands covering her right eye. Genevieve could feel the skin throb as it started to stretch and swell. "Holy shit," she muttered.

"Gen! Are you okay?" Maxine was at her side. Matthew, predictably, grabbed his coffee and left the room.

"Yeah, I think so." Genevieve started to move her hand away as Harper walked by the door.

"Genevieve?" Harper rushed to her. "Maxine? What happened?"

"She slammed her face into the chair!" Maxine tried her best to tamp down her amusement.

Harper stepped over and took a closer look at the chair, then at Genevieve, whose face was bright red. "There's eyeshadow on the chair," Harper said, pointing to the shimmering spot.

"I dropped my spoon…"

"I've got her, Maxine." Harper nodded at the older woman, dismissing her gently. Maxine left with a quiet laugh. Harper glared at Genevieve. "What really happened?"

"Exactly what Maxine said," Genevieve said with a shrug. *One day Harper will finally believe that this is my life.* "I dropped my spoon, and when I bent to pick it up, I hit the chair with my face."

"Move your hand away."

"I don't want to."

"Move your hand."

Genevieve dropped her hand slowly. She could tell by Harper's widening eyes and her slightly amused smile that she had done noticeable damage. "How bad is it?"

"On a scale of one to ten—one being a playground scuffle and ten being a heavyweight boxer—I'd say you're about an eleven."

"Oh no!" Genevieve covered her eye again and rushed to the bathroom. Once she was inside, she looked at her reflection and gasped. The skin of her upper eyelid was already purple, and she was bleeding from a small cut on the bone. She really was an eleven. Her eyes started to burn, but before she could start crying, Harper came through the door with an ice pack in hand.

"Hold still." She leaned Genevieve against the counter and nearly pinned her there with her body. Harper placed the ice pack over her eye gently and held it. "What am I going to do with you?"

"Wrap me in bubble wrap?" Genevieve said cheekily before wincing in pain. A headache started to blossom behind her eyes. "Or just keep me away from Clarissa."

"She did this?" Genevieve thought she looked confused at first, but when Harper's nostrils flared, she realized it was anger.

"No, but she made me drop my spoon because she stormed out of the break room after I said that I could see you hosting a party at your house. She hates me, and I have no idea why."

Harper pulled the ice pack away slowly and tilted Genevieve's head to the side.

Genevieve's head spun not only because of her injury but because Harper was so close. She could feel her breath against her mouth. Her hip bone pressed against Harper's thigh.

"She doesn't hate you, Genevieve." Harper smiled reassuringly and tucked a strand of Genevieve's hair behind her ear. "She hates that I like you."

Every thought Genevieve had avoided over the past couple of weeks came flooding back and engulfed her heart like a tidal wave. "Can I ask you something?"

"Anything."

"Why do you call me Genevieve and not Gen like everyone else?"

"You don't strike me as a Gen." Harper touched the swollen

skin by Genevieve's protruding brow tenderly. "Genevieve fit you perfectly from the moment I met you."

"Harper, I—"

The bathroom door swung open, and two chatty women entered, both nodding a polite hello to Harper. They were from advertising or finance or some department that rarely mingled with the writers. Genevieve grabbed the ice pack from Harper and left the bathroom with a meek thank you.

❖

"Chloe." Genevieve paced in front her bed. The plush carpeting tickled between her toes. "Chloe, I need your help," she said, gripping her phone tightly. Thinking these words and saying them aloud were two different things. "Chloe, I need your help because I think…" She paused to take a deep breath. "I *know* I'm attracted to my boss, and it goes beyond physical." Genevieve bit her lower lip. "Far beyond," she mumbled to herself. She'd said the words, now she just had to say them to someone.

Genevieve dialed. After the first ring, Chloe answered with a characteristic giggle. "This is new."

"What's new?"

"You calling me first. I'm used to being spoiled with texts or waiting for you to return one of my five calls."

"I'm sorry. Okay, I'm terrible and I know it, but that's kind of why I'm calling."

"Because you miss me and you hate yourself because of it?" Chloe laughed deeply. "Don't be silly, just make it up to me with a wild night out when I come to visit you." Genevieve didn't respond. "What's wrong?"

"I have to tell you something."

"Okay?"

"Well, three things actually."

"Spill! You're making me nervous!" Chloe shouted.

Genevieve shouted back. "I'm nervous!"

"Gen!"

"Fine!" Genevieve took two deep breaths and let them out slowly. "Chloe," she started just as she had rehearsed. "I want you to be my date for my work Christmas party, I'm attracted to my boss, and I gave myself a black eye at work yesterday."

"Oh my God, Genevieve Michelle Applegate!"

"I know." Genevieve fell onto her mattress and covered her eyes gingerly with her hand.

"No way."

"Yes way."

"How did you give yourself a black eye?" Chloe said, a fit of laughter taking over as soon as the words were out. Genevieve removed her hand from her face and stared at her ceiling, unblinking.

"That's all you heard?" Genevieve's question was wrapped in a whine.

Chloe continued to chuckle. "No, my dear Gen, but it's by far the most interesting part. I'm dying to know how you did it."

"How in the hell is that the most interesting part?"

"Because."

Genevieve pulled the phone away from her ear and frowned at the display. Chloe was so frustrating, she almost wanted to hang up on her, but Genevieve was desperate for her help.

Genevieve pinched the bridge of her nose and released a sigh. "Please elaborate."

"You've broken three toes, your wrist, have had more rug burns than any other person I know, and lost a lock of hair to a power drill, but you've never walked away from an incident with a black eye. Self-inflicted or not."

"Huh." Genevieve rifled through her many injuries, and Chloe was right. "It involves Clarissa, a spoon, and a poorly placed chair."

"Clarissa's the one who has it out for you for no real reason, right?"

"She has a reason, and it goes with the more important part of why I called you. Now, can we focus?"

"She has a thing for your boss, too?"

"Enough about Clarissa, I want to talk about me." Genevieve grew impatient. "Please."

"Oh, Gen. I don't know what you want me to say."

"Say anything. Tell me I'm crazy, tell me I love Jeremy, or tell me I've been lying for so long that I've convinced myself of these feelings." Genevieve swallowed the lump of fear in her throat before whispering, "Tell me you'll still love me."

"Genevieve, I'll love you even if you were calling to tell me you gave that black eye to a nun."

Genevieve laughed and released a long, relieved breath.

"I'm a little offended that you doubted that," Chloe said.

"I didn't, not really anyway. I wasn't thinking clearly."

"Obviously. You thought this news would be surprising for me."

"What do you mean?" Finally relaxed, Genevieve walked to her kitchen in search of a small snack and a drink.

"I'm talking about Becky in seventh grade and Mya from freshman year."

Genevieve thought back to those two ghosts. Silence engulfed her, as did a chill. Then she realized she was standing in front of the open refrigerator. Genevieve shook off her stupor and closed the door. "What are you getting at?"

"Remember the next door neighbor's babysitter? What was her name?"

"Margot." Genevieve had never felt that name did the beautiful brunette justice.

"You were insufferable when she was around, always wanting to play whatever game they were playing."

"She was older and cool."

"She was barely a year older, and I would catch you staring at her all the time. Mya, Becky, Margot—they're just the three I could think of. Gen, your boss is not your first girl crush. And before you say that what you're feeling is beyond a girl crush, that's because you're mature now. You finally understand what your heart is trying to tell you."

Genevieve stood nervously in her kitchen, toe tapping against the linoleum. "And Jeremy?"

"You're both comfortable, and it probably would've worked out if you didn't want more than what Milan had to offer. But for what it's worth, I don't think you're in love with him."

No drink. No snack. Genevieve's stomach twisted. She'd expected Chloe to be honest and forthcoming, but she wasn't expecting an entire upheaval of her life. Genevieve laughed mirthlessly. Of course she expected that. Chloe knew her better than she knew herself. You can't force self-denial onto your best friend.

"I love you, Chloe. Start packing for your visit. The party is the Friday before Christmas, and you'll need plenty of outfits to choose from."

"I wouldn't miss being your hot date for the world. I can't wait to meet Clarissa. She doesn't stand a chance against me."

"No, she doesn't. Thanks for everything."

"Anytime." Genevieve was about to disconnect the call

when she heard Chloe calling out to her. "Quick question. Does your boss have a date?"

Genevieve's stomach sank deeper, bottoming out as sickeningly low as it could go. Could Harper have a date? Some mystery woman draped on Harper's arm, stealing all of her attention?

"I...I don't know."

They ended their call shortly after. Genevieve carried the uneasy, uncertain feeling heavily as she shut off the lights in her apartment and climbed into bed. Sleep was the only thing that could stop her overactive imagination.

STEP FOURTEEN

If Necessary, Include a Partner

Genevieve stared at the rolling waves of the Atlantic. The rhythmic motion did little to spark her creative mind, but it did manage to soothe the rest of her. Since her conversation with Chloe, Genevieve had been more on edge than ever. She couldn't quite figure out why, but she had a feeling it had something to do with recognizing a truth while living a lie. She had avoided too much contact with Harper, needing the space to process her thoughts without any influence. Genevieve was amazed by how much pull those sterling eyes had and how much they warmed her even on the coldest day of the year. They could be the reason behind her every decision.

She was also fighting another war over two hundred miles away. Genevieve continued her nightly phone conversations with Jeremy, but they had very little to talk about, and neither could muster up interest in the other's halfhearted stories. She skipped the scheduled call last night, and she didn't feel guilty about it. Truthfully, she felt guiltier for not handing in her piece on time.

Genevieve saw Dana approaching quickly and quietly, but she wasn't going to let the stealthy woman get the best of her again. She spun around and nearly shouted, "Dana!"

Dana jumped back and yelped. She readjusted her hair before nodding slightly at Genevieve. "I deserved that," she said with a small smile.

Genevieve barely contained her proud laughter. In the distance, she could see Maxine giving her a thumbs up. "What's up?"

"Ms. Davies would like to see you." Genevieve's smile fell. "She's probably a little worried that she hasn't received your piece yet."

"Oh." Genevieve waved Dana's relayed concern off. "Tell her it's almost done."

"She'll be very happy to hear that." Dana smiled politely, and when Genevieve turned to leave, she said, "From you."

Genevieve forced a tight-lipped smile. "Fine," she said with a clenched jaw.

The walk from the ocean view to Harper's office was a short one, and Genevieve wished she had at least one or two small distractions to detain her, but she didn't even see a paper clip on the floor to pick up. She missed Harper's smile and the gentle cadence of her words, but she was trying to protect both Harper and herself.

She stood outside Harper's closed office door and checked her appearance. Her navy blue blouse was tucked neatly into her beige tweed skirt. She straightened the large bow at the neckline of her shirt, a detail she loved at first but that strangled her now. She shook off her discomfort and knocked before opening the door enough to peek inside.

"Harper?"

"Genevieve!" Harper looked up from her paperwork with a vibrant smile. "Come in."

"Your bounty hunter told me you wanted to see me."

"Ah yes. I messaged you, but when I didn't get a reply I decided to send Dana for you. She's effective."

"That she is." Genevieve took a seat across from her and tried not to fall into her gentle gaze. "What can I do for you?"

"I just wanted to—" Harper paused and looked just over Genevieve's shoulder before she stood and closed the office door again. When she came back, she took a seat beside Genevieve instead of her usual spot behind the desk. Genevieve grew nervous. Harper sat at the edge of her seat and leaned forward, minimizing the space between them before speaking quietly. "I just wanted to check in."

"I know my piece is a day late, but the first draft is just about done. Everything's fine." Genevieve should've tried to lean back and away from Harper's body to rein in her sanity, but Genevieve knew if she moved at all, it'd be toward Harper.

Harper's head fell. "I had a feeling you'd say that, and as much as I want to believe you, I don't." She looked up at Genevieve again. "It's like someone else is writing your stuff lately."

"I'm just a little off."

"And you're not talking," Harper said sullenly. "At least not to me. Did I do something?"

"What? No." Genevieve reached out and grabbed Harper's hand. "It's just..." Genevieve struggled to find the right words. She didn't want to complicate the situation by lying, but she wasn't ready to offer the truth. She saw the twinkling lights outside the window. "The holiday season is always a lot for me. Christmas is great once it's here, but the lead-up is overwhelming." Genevieve didn't want Harper to question her anymore, so she turned the conversation back to work. "Has my column been lacking?"

"No, it's not that." Harper traced the delicate bones of Genevieve's hand with her thumb, but she politely pulled her hand back to her lap. Harper looked a bit disappointed but covered it quickly by getting back to business. "It just seems a bit less personal, that's all. I don't think any readers picked up on that. It could've just been me."

"I can promise you that with Christmas coming up, I'll be getting very personal."

"How's your eye?" Harper sat forward again, this time reaching out and tracing along Genevieve's bruised brow bone. Genevieve sucked in a sharp breath. Her eyes fluttered closed at the delicate touch.

Genevieve didn't understand how the barely-there contact could affect her so. Why was her writing so impersonal lately? Because Genevieve couldn't put this feeling into written words without having to explain so much more.

"It's okay," Genevieve said, struggling against the desire to lean into the touch. "The bruise is getting darker, but it's not as sore. I can wiggle my eyebrows now without wanting to cry."

Harper laughed when she did so. "Good. We have to make sure that skill is never lost." Harper went back to her seat behind her desk. "Are you ready for the party tomorrow night?" She shuffled a few papers before sitting.

"Are *you* ready? You're the host, after all."

Harper waved her off. "Oh, please. The caterers do all the hard work. I just supply the venue."

"I'm looking forward to it. I've heard your Christmas parties are not to be missed."

"Whatever you heard is true, good or bad."

Silence stretched on. Genevieve wanted to prolong the conversation just so she could enjoy Harper's company a bit longer. She had avoided her boss for days, and now she wanted to drink up their time together like she was dehydrated. Harper flipped a switch in her. One minute she could be so cool and in control, and the next she was a mess of ardor and want. Genevieve felt like she was suffering from emotional whiplash.

"I'll let you get back to work—"

"Would you like to get dinner—"

Harper and Genevieve spoke at the same time.

Genevieve blushed at Harper's unexpected invitation. As much as she wanted to accept and ask whether the outing was work-related or not, Genevieve's plans were already set.

"I can't, I'm sorry."

"Don't be, it was very last minute. Maybe some other time." Harper's voice hardened slightly, but Genevieve clung to the hint of hopefulness she heard in it.

"Absolutely." Genevieve stood and walked to the door, when she turned back, Harper was smiling. She leaned against the doorway and bit her lip. "See you around, boss." She winked before walking back to her desk.

That short time spent with Harper renewed Genevieve's waning writer's heart. She had a different focus on writing a piece about being single during the holidays now, and she was able to finish just a little before four thirty.

"Going into the week-long stretch of holiday celebrations without someone to love may not be easy," she read aloud, "but when you already have your sights set on achievable resolutions, loneliness dissipates and optimism shines brighter than holiday lights." Genevieve sat back with a smile of satisfaction. She sent the final product to Harper and gathered her things before bidding her coworkers good-bye and running out the door.

The holiday season always went by quicker than she really preferred. Genevieve missed her childhood, when making it to winter break was a struggle and the mere thought of Christmas morning felt like decades away. Now Genevieve panicked about how she could fit everything on her to-do list into one evening. She fidgeted by the window in her bedroom and waited to catch a glimpse of Chloe's car. They had to shop, they surely needed manicures and pedicures, and they needed to put together the perfect ensemble for Genevieve to wear to the party. Genevieve was fairly certain Harper was interested in her, and she needed to make sure it stayed that way until she cleaned up the mess she had created.

Shortly after six o'clock, Chloe's car crawled down the street, turned around, and went the other direction. Finding street parking in front of Genevieve's apartment was always a struggle. Genevieve imagined how much Chloe was likely cursing. She laughed and grabbed her coat, wanting to see her as soon as possible. She ran down the stairs in a rush and came to a stop on the small porch of her building. Chloe had finally found a spot and was approaching, her hands filled with bags of all kinds.

"Are you moving in?"

"You wish." Chloe dropped a large, overfilled duffel bag at Genevieve's feet and handed her a nondescript white box with ribbon tied around it. "For you."

"Is this...?" Genevieve said, even though she recognized the blank box and plain ribbon.

"Doughnuts from Randy's? Of course. There's a whole dozen in there, so try to save me one."

"No promises."

"Don't even think about it," Chloe said. Genevieve rolled her eyes and took hold of one end of the heavy duffel. "Don't roll your eyes at me. Nice shiner, by the way."

"You should've seen it last week."

"I wish I had, but you refused to send pictures."

Together they hoisted everything up the stairs into Genevieve's apartment. After Chloe's arms were free, she wrapped them around Genevieve in a robust hug. In that familiar embrace, whatever weak control Genevieve had over her emotions crumbled. So many months of lying, tiptoeing along the truth, and using avoidance as a lifesaving tactic had worn Genevieve thin.

"You're okay," Chloe whispered as she rubbed soothing circles on her friend's back. "Let it out, you're okay."

They sat on the couch and talked without a phone in hand or needing to rush off for the first time since Genevieve had moved to New Jersey. Genevieve shared every detail of her feelings between bites of fried and glazed dough.

"What do you plan on telling Harper?" Chloe asked.

Genevieve discarded a small bit of uneaten doughnut back into the box and licked her fingertips. "I don't know." She threw her head back into the cushions. "Just like how I have no idea what to tell Jeremy."

"Screw Jeremy."

"I thought you liked Jeremy."

"I like him plenty." Chloe gathered her long, dark hair into a ponytail. "He's been one of my closest guy friends since grade school. I just never liked him for you."

"Why didn't you say anything?" Genevieve pulled the throw pillow out from behind her back and hit her friend with it.

Chloe shielded herself. "Because I thought you were happy!"

"What changed?"

"I see you now, and even though you're going through a lot of shit at the moment, there's something different. Good different. You sparkle."

"I sparkle?" Genevieve raised her eyebrow.

"When you talk about Harper or *Out Shore,* the sparkle is in your voice, and now that I'm looking at you, it's in your eyes, too."

"That's the stupidest thing I've ever heard."

"Stupid or not, it's true. Now, let's go." Chloe smacked

Genevieve's thigh and stood. "We have shopping to do, and you owe me a night out."

"It won't be wild," Genevieve said. Trying to accomplish anything after a day of work felt impossible, and her lack of emotional strength wasn't helping matters. "First we find our dresses for tomorrow night, and then I'll take you to a bar I've been hearing a lot about. I can use the visit for my next piece."

"Oh!" Chloe clapped excitedly. "A gay bar?"

"Yes, Chloe, a gay bar."

Chloe's squeal of delight hurt Genevieve's ears.

❖

"A lot of people from work come here to unwind," Genevieve shouted into Chloe's ear. They leaned against the bar and watched as men and women of different ages, races, and styles milled about, chatting and smiling.

"Recognize anyone?" Chloe said. Genevieve looked around and shook her head. They drank without speaking for some time, each just taking in the surroundings. "Anyone catching your eye?" Chloe said with a wry smile.

"The last thing I need is for anyone else to catch my eye!" Genevieve pushed her friend and took a sip of her cold beer.

"What does Harper look like?"

"You'll meet her tomorrow night."

"Does she look like her?" Chloe nodded toward the heavily tattooed bartender with short bleached hair. Genevieve raised her eyebrows and shook her head. "What about her?" Chloe gestured at a feminine woman with long dark hair and perfectly crafted winged eyeliner. The woman was gorgeous, but so far from Harper Genevieve thought the comparison was pure comedy, and she laughed outright.

"Not even close."

"Then tell me."

"No one here looks like her." She thought of Harper's style and her smile. Genevieve had never met anyone who could compare to her. She stared down at her beer bottle and smiled before speaking. "She has a very unique look, very androgynous."

"Like boyish?"

"But soft. She dresses *so* well—fitted suits and shirts. She's always put together. You can tell she was an athlete or at least works out quite a bit because she's pretty built, but not too big." Genevieve sighed and rolled her eyes. She wasn't describing Harper well at all. "It's her eyes that get me," she said so quietly that Chloe had to lean in. "I swear I lose hours every time I look in them."

"Color?"

"Gray."

"Height?"

"Tall."

"Hair?"

"Dark and short, always in place," Genevieve said.

Chloe took a sip of her beer, seemingly finished with her rapid-fire questioning. "She sounds attractive," Chloe said indifferently.

"She is." Genevieve pictured Harper standing in her office, hands buried deep in the pockets of her suit pants, pulled tight against her muscular buttocks. Her dress shirt would most definitely be blue, maybe a cobalt or royal to bring out her eyes. She'd have her sleeves rolled up to mid-forearm, showing off the start of strong arms and a fancy large watch. Whenever Genevieve thought about Harper, she was smiling. The top button of her collared shirt was always left open and the rest would fit the curves of her torso so well. "She really is." Genevieve swallowed roughly.

"I'll be the judge of that tomorrow night." Chloe tapped their beer bottles together.

Step Fifteen

Don't Hesitate to Let Loose

Genevieve stared out the car window at Harper's house. Every light was on and people filled the main rooms. She was looking, but she wasn't really seeing. She was imagining the possible conversations and confrontations that could take place, preparing answers and appropriate comebacks should she need them.

"If I had known we'd be sitting in the car all night," Chloe said, "I would've worn pajamas instead of a dress."

"Don't rush me."

"Well, I'm going." Chloe opened her car door and got out.

Genevieve grabbed her small clutch and tightened the scarf around her neck, catching up to Chloe just as she pushed the doorbell.

"Chloe! What the hell?" Genevieve shoved her friend just enough to make Chloe wobble and laugh.

"Like you were planning on leaving the car!"

Genevieve rolled her eyes. "You are such a pain in my—"

The door opened and Dana smiled at her. "Gen. Come in! Everyone else is already here." Dana ushered Genevieve and Chloe inside, taking their coats and stowing them in a closet along the way.

Chloe leaned into Genevieve and asked in a whisper, "*This* is Dana? I thought you said she's a robot."

"She is," Genevieve insisted, "at least at work she is. I've never seen her in a social setting." They followed Dana into Harper's large, open kitchen, running into Genevieve's friends from work, all gathered by the glass doors looking out into the backyard.

"Genevieve Applegate!" Matthew shouted and waved her over.

"Hey, guys," Genevieve said shyly. Parties weren't usually her thing, but having Chloe around helped her relax. She looked at Maxine and the short blonde standing close to her side. "Maxine, is this the infamous Connie?" Genevieve smiled politely.

"Guilty," Connie said and reached out to take Genevieve's hand. "You must be Genevieve. Maxine said you were from Pennsylvania and that it showed."

Genevieve grinned. "And what exactly does that mean?"

"You're the purest definition of the girl next door," Maxine said. "There's not many country-looking women in this area."

"Or natural strawberry-blondes," Matthew said with a wink. He pointed to Genevieve's black dress, long-sleeved and knee-length with a lace overlay that showed skin everywhere but from bust to knee. "Looking good, by the way. This is much better than the prudish outfits you wear to work."

Genevieve's sarcastic retort was on the tip of her tongue when Chloe cleared her throat. Remembering her manners, Genevieve introduced her friend. "This is my very best friend, Chloe, and she has been dying to meet you all." She pushed Chloe forward gently. While Chloe shook each hand and exchanged pleasantries, Clarissa walked up with an attractive woman on her arm.

"Doing introductions without me?" Clarissa said with a cocky smile.

"If it hadn't taken you fifteen minutes to get a drink, we wouldn't have," Matthew said.

Clarissa stared at Chloe. "And who is this?"

"I'm Chloe," she said, squaring her shoulders, "and you must be Clarissa."

Clarissa's mouth turned up at the corner, and she looked at the woman by her side. "Alison, these are my coworkers." Clarissa introduced everyone by name and looked at Chloe again. "Are you the friend Gen was in love with for so long?"

"I am." Chloe wrapped her arm around her waist and pulled Genevieve closer. "And I'm still mad at myself for not reciprocating. Gen's hot."

"So are you," Clarissa said.

"You should probably focus on your date." Chloe nodded toward Alison.

Genevieve laughed outright. She waited for a sarcastic quip from Clarissa, but it never came. Instead, Clarissa smirked at Harper standing just behind at the kitchen counter, an odd look on her face.

"I guess she's just as surprised by you bringing a date as we are," Clarissa said quietly enough for only Genevieve and Chloe to hear.

"Ignore her," Chloe said. "I think it's time for me to finally meet Harper."

As they approached Harper, Genevieve took in her appearance. She wore charcoal dress pants and a burgundy sweater like no one else. An irrational sense of pride swelled in Genevieve's chest. Harper wasn't hers to be proud of, but introducing Chloe to her when she looked this good was incredibly satisfying.

"Harper," Genevieve said, "this is my best friend, Chloe. Chloe, this is my boss, Harper."

"Nice to finally meet you," Chloe said.

Harper cocked her head. "Finally? Has Genevieve been talking about me?" Harper's question was mostly directed to Genevieve, but Chloe answered nonetheless.

"She talks about you—"

"And the magazine and work a lot," Genevieve said. Harper hummed in understanding, but Genevieve saw the amusement shining in her light eyes.

"Are you two old friends?"

Chloe laughed. "*Very* old friends. We've been best friends since Milan Elementary."

Harper smiled and excused herself, claiming she had more guests to tend to. Genevieve watched Harper walk away with a forlorn expression.

"What was that about?"

"They all think I'm in love with you. Harper does too." Genevieve shook her head and looked around for where the drinks were being hidden. She desperately needed one now. "Matthew asked me if I had ever fallen for a friend and I said yes and it was you, and Harper heard me." Genevieve huffed. "Another lie!"

"And here I thought we were living a true, unrequited love story." Genevieve shot Chloe a stern glare. "Sorry, back to Harper." They watched as Harper disappeared into a room just off the dining room. "You said she was attractive, and you weren't kidding. She's gorgeous. She's really sexy, too."

Genevieve frowned.

"Well, go and clear this up!" Chloe shoved Genevieve toward the dining room.

"I don't want to leave you."

"Please, I'll be fine on my own. I'll probably have two new best friends by the time you get back from canoodling."

"Fine." Genevieve took a deep breath, steadying her nerves.

After keeping her distance for some time and now appearing quite cozy with a supposed "old flame," she was afraid this would be the final nail in the coffin of their relationship. Genevieve never expected her flippant lie about Chloe to have such repercussions. Genevieve raised her shaking hand and knocked on the door before cracking it open.

Harper sat behind a large desk. Her home office was almost a carbon copy of the office she occupied at *Out Shore,* except this space felt much more intimate. Genevieve smiled at Harper shyly as she closed the door behind her. She swallowed dryly. "Working during your own party?"

"Not really." Harper pushed away from the desk. "Just enjoying the quiet. I'm not much of a party person."

"Me either." She needed to bite the bullet and just talk. "Harper, I just wanted to explain. Chloe isn't—"

Harper stood and held up her hand. "You don't owe me an explanation."

"I do. At least I hope I do, I think there's a reason why I should…" Genevieve's heart started to thunder in her chest as she stepped closer to Harper. "Everyone was talking about falling in love. I'm just a girl from Small Town, USA. I didn't have anything juicy to share, so I made it up. Chloe and I have been best friends since the first grade, *platonic* best friends."

"You don't have to lie to fit in around here, especially not with me," Harper said softly, unknowingly twisting the knife of guilt in Genevieve's chest. "I apologize for thinking the worst," she said, licking her lips and crossing her arms over her chest. "Genevieve, I have a hard time trusting my feelings. You—this is a first for me in a long time."

"What do you mean?" Genevieve said.

"I was married once."

"M-married?"

"Till death do us part, and I was crazy about her. She was everything I thought I wanted in a wife." Harper's head fell back, and she stared at the ceiling as she laughed wryly. "We were together for two years before my uncle died, and then I was grief-stricken and in charge of this magazine suddenly. The rest of my life was moving forward, and I wanted my relationship to as well. We had a great wedding and an even better honeymoon. We settled into life as a married couple and it didn't seem like anything had changed. But as it turned out, we were both completely different people." When Harper looked at Genevieve again, her normally bright eyes were dull and misty.

"What happened?"

Harper's shoulders fell sadly. "She wasn't ready to get married, to make that kind of commitment to one person, but she didn't know how to turn down my proposal. I'm sure you could imagine how hard it is to say no to someone who's grieving." Harper swallowed harshly and cleared her throat. "We were married for less than two months before the fighting became nonstop, and less than six before she cheated on me."

"Harper, I am so sorry." Genevieve placed her hand on Harper's arm.

"For the longest time I was afraid of getting close to someone again, to invest those kind of feelings in another person. I didn't trust my judgment after that," she said in a gravelly voice. "But how I reacted in there? And this feeling

I have in the pit of my stomach every time I'm around you? I think it's time."

Genevieve was floored. Her heart was racing, pumping excitement through her limbs. She vibrated with happiness and amazement that Harper felt the same way. She hadn't imagined the chemistry between them. Clarity and certainty washed over her. She could still lead with her heart, but her life would be nothing but the truth from now on.

"Harper, I need you to know—"

A sharp knock at the door echoed through the room. Genevieve stepped away from Harper, irritated at the interruption.

"Harper?" Matthew hollered through the door. "Do you have more white wine?"

"Yes. I'll bring some out in a minute." Harper looked at Genevieve. "I'm being a terrible host. I guess we should get back to the party."

"I have so much to tell you," Genevieve said, not bothering to hide her irritation.

"There's always time to talk, but there's only one Christmas party here a year." Harper placed a gentle hand low on Genevieve's back and escorted her from the room.

They walked just into the large doorway of the kitchen, then Matthew stopped them with a loud wolf whistle. When Genevieve turned back to Matthew, he pointed to the mistletoe hanging above them.

"Huh," Harper said as she looked up, her mouth slightly agape. "I forgot I put that there." She looked at Genevieve with a mischievous glint in her eye. Genevieve was sure Harper was lying, but the rest of the crowd started to egg them on. When Harper shrugged, Genevieve stepped forward.

Genevieve stood flush against her and placed her hands

high on Harper's chest. She looked into her eyes and then at her full glistening lips. She didn't give a damn that she was about to kiss Harper in front of her peers, she just needed to taste her for the first time.

Harper leaned in close enough for the tip of her nose to graze Genevieve's. Harper's breath ghosted across her mouth, and Genevieve licked her lips in anticipation. Genevieve closed the small distance between them, pressing her lips against Harper's.

Genevieve marveled at the softness of her mouth as their lips melded. What amazed her more was how Harper was soft *everywhere*: her lips, her skin, and the way she held Genevieve's waist with gentle assertion. She forgot about the prying eyes surrounding them, and she parted her lips, wanting so badly to deepen the kiss. But Harper pecked her and pulled away. Genevieve slowly opened her eyes, Harper scratching the back of her neck bashfully. The sound of glass shattering in the distance pulled her completely from her daze.

"Well, well…" Matthew said as he walked past them and sipped his wine.

"Let me go check on that, and we'll talk. I promise." Harper winked and ran off toward the sound of the accident.

Genevieve stood frozen, unsure as to whether the kiss had happened or if she had imagined it, but Chloe's broad grin clued Genevieve into the reality and the enormity of it.

"You need to talk to Jeremy."

Genevieve's glee turned grim quickly.

STEP SIXTEEN

Out with the Old

The guilt Genevieve felt at fleeing Harper's Christmas party immediately after their kiss was nothing compared to the guilt that had been haunting her for months. She had been lying to Harper day after day, falling for someone while she was in a committed relationship with Jeremy. Sneaking out of a party without saying good-bye was the least of her worries. Genevieve knew she had to make a change. When Harper texted her the morning after the party, she explained she was heading back to Pennsylvania for a couple of days.

She drove mile after mile, heavy snowflakes falling onto her windshield in intermittent showers. Genevieve hated driving in the snow. She had once loved the magical feel of it, the way she could imagine traveling through space at warp speed. But after hearing one too many horror stories, Genevieve was afraid of slick conditions and potential accidents. Why couldn't she be that cautious with other aspects of her life?

Genevieve pulled up in front of Jeremy's small home. He had been renovating the place, but much like everything else in Jeremy's life, he worked very slowly at it. His truck was in the driveway so Genevieve knew he was likely home, which relieved and terrified her.

She had no idea what to say. She had no real experience with breakups, and since they hadn't been speaking regularly, Genevieve wasn't even sure how she should approach the topic. Were they still together? Genevieve was unsure of everything except that she needed to end it with Jeremy so she could work toward a beginning with Harper. Genevieve was willing to do anything just to kiss Harper again without guilt weighing her down.

Genevieve quickly noted the difference in the air as she exited her car. The breeze was devoid of the salty tang she was now used to, and she missed its taste. She jogged up the front steps and held her puffy nylon jacket tight around her. It must've been ten to fifteen degrees colder in this part of Pennsylvania, and the chill matched Genevieve's own bitterness. She knocked even though she had a key, in spite of the fact that this house was supposed to be the one they shared after holy matrimony.

Jeremy's footsteps were heavy as he approached the door. He swung it open with a disgruntled frown. "Gen?" Confusion riddled his bearded face. His appearance was more unkempt than usual, something that happened when Genevieve wasn't around him for a few days.

"Hey, Jeremy," Genevieve said awkwardly. They stared at one another for a few moments before a gust of wind whipped around Genevieve. "Can I come in?"

"Yeah! Of course!" Jeremy stepped aside and ushered Genevieve in. "I'm sorry, I was just so surprised to see you. I didn't think you were coming home until tomorrow."

Genevieve removed her jacket and placed it across the arm of the couch. "I should've called."

"I love surprises." Jeremy wrapped his arms around her. "I get to see you for Christmas Eve and Christmas Day. Best surprise ever." He leaned down and kissed her softly.

Genevieve wanted to pull back immediately, feeling a sense of betrayal toward Harper, which was telling since she hadn't even thought of Jeremy during her mistletoe kiss. Genevieve stayed in the embrace, searching her memory for a time when Jeremy elicited a feeling like Harper did. She came up empty.

Genevieve pulled back and smiled, but the curl of her lips was closer to a grimace. "I came by because we need to talk." Genevieve rolled her eyes at her own cliché. "I want to talk about not talking."

"You want to talk about not talking?" Jeremy sat heavily on the sofa, his basketball shorts riding high on his hairy thighs.

Genevieve was already getting irritated. One sentence in, and she was struggling with how to say what she was feeling. She sat beside him stiffly. "We haven't been talking at all."

"You've been busy."

Genevieve was taken aback. "I never said that."

"You didn't have to. Every time I called, you barely had time to talk, and you'd always call late at night. We'd be half asleep. We didn't do any talking then." Jeremy was right. That's exactly how the majority of phone calls were since she had moved to New Jersey.

"I guess what I'm about to say won't be a surprise, then." Genevieve waited, hoping Jeremy would know where this conversation was going. She didn't want to play a guessing game, but she didn't want to say the words either. She nervously pulled the cuffs of her long-sleeved thermal over her hands as she waited.

It took a few moments, but realization slowly dawned on Jeremy's face. He sat forward, leaning a bit closer to Genevieve in the process. "Gen, do you—I mean…" He cleared his throat and shook his head. When he looked at Genevieve again, he wore a broad smile. "Do you want to get married?"

Genevieve's mouth fell open. "What?"

"Are you ready to get married? Is that it? Because I'm ready, Gen. I have been."

"No, that's not it." Genevieve pinched the bridge of her nose. She was sure this couldn't get any harder, but it had.

"Are you moving home? Don't feel bad about that. It's hard for a lot of people to make it on their own." Jeremy took Genevieve's hand, and that contact sparked her irritation into full-blown anger. Her life didn't revolve around Jeremy. It never did, and it never would.

"No!" She pulled back and straightened her shoulders. "It's neither, Jeremy. I came here because I think it's time for us to end whatever it is that's still going on between us."

Genevieve waited again, knowing he couldn't misinterpret that. She was prepared for any reaction except the laughter that bubbled up from him.

"You're breaking up with me because we don't talk every night? That's ridiculous. Do you want something to drink?" He walked into the kitchen. His nonchalance shocked Genevieve.

"That's not why. That's just evidence that it's the right decision."

"Then why?" Jeremy said when he came back with a beer and sat down. He still appeared unfazed, as if this was just another argument where he'd call Genevieve irrational and they'd walk away from an unresolved problem and be back at square one.

"Because we're different people now," she said, looking around the disheveled home. "This is you. This isn't me."

"Are you too good, is that it?"

"No, I'm not too good for anyone or anything." Genevieve dropped her head momentarily, thinking she might not be good enough for the future she was hoping for. "Our lives went in opposite directions." Genevieve struggled to keep her hold on what little patience she had left.

"You've changed," Jeremy said, pointing an accusatory finger. "I haven't."

"After ten years, don't you think that's a problem?"

"Is there someone else?" Jeremy placed his beer on a small wooden side table with a loud thud. "It has to get lonely in Jersey all by yourself. Is that it? Little Genevieve Applegate spread her wings and her legs?"

"Excuse me?" Genevieve's nostrils flared. "Don't you dare talk to me like that."

"Look me in the eye and tell me I'm wrong."

Genevieve stared back into Jeremy's eyes, eyes she barely recognized. "I didn't look for someone else," she said against her better judgment.

"You're avoiding the question. *Is* there someone else?"

Genevieve clenched her jaw. *No more lies.* "I have feelings for someone else, yes."

"Who?"

"I'm not answering that."

"Tell me who, dammit!" Jeremy shouted. "Who is he and how did you meet him? You tell me how busy you are, but you had time to go out and meet someone new?"

"I didn't go looking—"

"Well, you couldn't have met him at work because you're surrounded by a bunch of homos."

"Jeremy, stop." She took a deep breath, trying her best to rein in her anger and tamp down her nerves. She felt dizzy, her palms were sweaty, and she started to shake.

"Unless he's a switch-hitter." Jeremy laughed at his own joke. "Or maybe a lezzy swooped in to steal you from me." His punch line went unacknowledged, but the silence was thick, and Genevieve never looked up from her lap. "Holy shit."

"I didn't expect it."

"Get out." Jeremy walked to the door and opened it before Genevieve had the chance to get her coat on.

"Despite what you may think of me, I am sorry."

"I said get out." Jeremy's face hardened.

Genevieve gathered herself and fought to keep her tears at bay. She knew the breakup wouldn't be easy, but she hadn't planned for this. She stepped onto the front porch and welcomed the fresh, biting air against her wet cheeks. Before she made it to the steps, Jeremy spoke up.

"You're throwing away everything we had and everything we planned for some dyke."

Genevieve paused and closed her eyes. She spun around and got in Jeremy's face. "She's a part of the life I always dreamed of, a life that's so much bigger than anything you could've given me." She wiped away a stubborn tear. "Goodbye, Jeremy."

When Genevieve went back to her car, she smiled at the freedom she felt. Instead of a broken heart, Genevieve felt open to endless possibilities.

❖

She traditionally celebrated Christmas Eve at her mother's house, and she was expected to arrive in an hour. Genevieve took a deep breath, knowing that she'd have to be her most creative self to avoid a conversation about why Jeremy wouldn't be joining them. The prospect of a holiday with family *explaining* a breakup seemed much more daunting than the breakup itself. Genevieve had no idea how her mother would react to the news. Sandra wasn't the one in the relationship with Jeremy, but Genevieve cared about whether her mother approved of her biggest life decisions.

Genevieve considered all the ways she had changed since moving to New Jersey. She had fallen easily into an independent life, she felt inspired every day at work and even at night when she wrote for more personal reasons, and she had acknowledged and accepted this dormant part of her heart. That was the most exciting and surprising, not because she was recognizing a new facet to her sexuality, but because she never knew she was capable of this desire to be with another person.

She finally understood what romance writers drabbled on about and how romantic movies were always such a hit. Those feelings were real and addicting. Genevieve also realized why writing engagement announcements never came easily for her. In her mind they were fiction. But love and romance and truly being gaga for your significant other wasn't fiction at all. It was just a matter of finding the right person to fawn over.

Genevieve parked and sat quietly in her car while she gathered her thoughts. Her mother stood on the front porch waving to her, wearing the same reindeer apron she'd worn for every other Christmas Genevieve could remember.

"After the holidays I'll tell Harper everything," she said aloud. "I'll tell her I lied to get a job, but that it doesn't matter now because it turned out to be the truth." Genevieve closed her eyes and counted to ten before climbing out of the car, wholly unprepared for Christmas with her family.

STEP SEVENTEEN

In with the New

Genevieve survived Christmas. She was both surprised and delighted by how easily the two days passed. Sandra had asked about Jeremy only once and didn't say anything when Genevieve told her he had his own family gathering to attend. Sandra seemed to be more interested in Genevieve's Jersey life and the job she was so fond of. Genevieve spent most of her time home talking about how much she enjoyed both her life and position at *Out Shore*. She even went as far as mentioning the title of the publication multiple times, no longer caring if someone discovered it was a gay magazine. They'd all find out soon enough.

Now, as the final hours of the year dwindled away, Genevieve was home typing away on her keyboard. She could've done anything for New Year's Eve, but she'd opted to spend as much time on herself and at home as possible. The New Year was going to bring big things for Genevieve Applegate, good or bad, and she was set on preparing for it.

Her phone chimed and distracted Genevieve from the piece she was working on. She was trying to capture her and Chloe's night out at a local gay bar as honestly as possible. She was writing a seemingly innocent piece, but the raw emotion poured from her as she recounted the way she compared every face there to the one person who captured her attention, the one person who also happened to be unattainable at the moment. Her phone chimed a second time and Genevieve grumbled as she reached for it.

Harper had messaged her twice. Genevieve's eyes went wide at the six-letter name lighting up her screen. The first message was a short greeting, but the message that followed made her smile.

Any big plans for New Years?

No, Genevieve typed out. *Home alone and working hard to satisfy my boss.*

That sounds terrible. Someone should have a talk with this boss of yours. Genevieve smiled at her phone, and before she could type out a response, another message came through. *I'd offer to do it for you, but I'm busy tonight.*

Genevieve frowned at her phone. Why would Harper message her just to brag about her plans for New Year's Eve?

Genevieve?

Yes?

Please open your door.

A knock followed Harper's last message and Genevieve jumped. She checked her appearance briefly. She was wearing a tank, zip-up hoodie, and yoga pants, hardly an appropriate outfit for entertaining company on New Year's Eve. But she didn't have a choice. Her heart was speeding and her stomach was doing the funny flips she had associated with Harper. She opened the door. Genevieve smiled so brightly, her cheeks hurt.

"Hey," Harper said.

"Hey." Genevieve fiddled with the hair piled haphazardly atop her head. "I obviously wasn't expecting anyone."

"You look perfect," Harper said, holding up a large, stuffed plastic bag. "May I come in? I brought dinner."

Genevieve stepped aside. "Of course. What's in the bag?"

"A lot of Chinese food." Harper laughed and set down the bag before removing her jacket. "I hope you're hungry, and I hope you don't mind company. I figured it was the perfect time to return the favor for Thanksgiving. Except this is definitely not homemade."

"I would never mind your company," Genevieve said. "But I am surprised that you don't have actual big plans."

"I gave up New Year's parties a long time ago," Harper said as she set out their dinner, "but I didn't want to be alone tonight. Not because I'm lonely or sad, but because I knew there's someone I'd rather be with." Genevieve blushed as Harper smiled.

"Smooth talker."

Harper smirked. "A little bit of everything? Let's see, we've got General Tsao's chicken, moo goo gai pan, pork egg foo yung, fried rice with shrimp, lo mein, and my favorite— mixed vegetables in brown sauce, extra mushrooms."

Genevieve shuddered slightly in obvious disgust.

"Not a fan?"

"I used to be, but my grandmother served us a feast of wild mushrooms one time and almost killed us all. I've never been so sick in my life, and I haven't enjoyed a mushroom since. Not even on pizza."

Harper stayed silent and just smiled at Genevieve softly.

"What?" Genevieve said.

"Nothing, I just—" Harper licked her lips and looked almost nervous. "I'm just really happy I decided to do this, to come here, I mean." She cleared her throat. "You have plates and knives and forks, right?"

Genevieve had never seen Harper so unsure and bashful. This side of her was so endearing, Genevieve fell even harder for the other woman. She was afraid that an awkwardness would come between them, and she was terrified Harper would dismiss their kiss as holiday tradition rather than something bigger.

"Me too," Genevieve said. The simple words seemed to appease Harper, who finished plating their takeout feast.

Harper and Genevieve ate in companionable silence. Genevieve flipped through the channels on her TV, grateful she had decided to keep her cable hooked up in spite of rarely using it. They had decided against the usual New Year's Eve programs, not interested in popular music groups and young personalities rambling on about how wonderful the city was in the winter.

"Keep the city and give me the beach any day," Harper said around a forkful of lo mein.

"Keep the city *and* the country." She picked up her empty plate and stood. "Need anything?"

Harper handed over her plate. "Please take this from me. If I eat another bite, I'll have to resolve to lose twenty-five pounds."

Genevieve carried their dishes into the kitchen and cleaned up slowly. She grabbed two beers from the refrigerator and walked back to the living room, indulging in the sight of Harper lounging casually across the sofa.

Harper's sleeves were rolled up to mid-forearm, and the button of her jeans was undone—showing exactly how much she had enjoyed her meal. Harper's shoes were off, showing her bright patterned socks, and she was yawning widely.

"Do you want this or will it put you to sleep?" Genevieve teased.

"Thanks." Harper took the beer and settled back. "I'm not young like you. Midnight is a foreign concept for me at this point."

Genevieve settled into the corner of the couch, noticing

how Harper had managed to occupy more space. She was either getting very comfortable or trying to get closer. "You really need to stop talking about your age like that," Genevieve said. "You're not old, and I'm not a baby. We're just...us."

"Us," Harper said, turning turned her head to Genevieve. A strand of strawberry-blond hair had escaped Genevieve's bun, and Harper tucked it behind her ear. The delicate touch sent a shiver down Genevieve's spine. Harper rested her head on the back cushions, her eyes never straying far from Genevieve's face. She yawned again.

"What can I do to help keep you awake?" Genevieve hadn't meant for her words to be so suggestive. "A movie?" Genevieve said quickly.

"A movie sounds perfect."

Genevieve checked her cable guide and selected the first one that caught her eye. "I love this one."

Harper squinted at the bright screen to read the title. "*Thongs of the Undead*? Are you serious?"

"What? It's a cult classic. I used to watch this at every sleepover I had in high school."

"And parents were okay with that?"

"What they didn't know didn't hurt them." Genevieve winked and tossed the remote onto her small coffee table. The mindless film was more of a comedy than a horror movie. Harper laughed and made comments about the film's poor quality. Genevieve loved sharing something so ordinary with her.

Approximately an hour before midnight, Harper fell asleep against Genevieve's side. Harper's slightly parted lips and twitching eyelids made her look peaceful. Genevieve could either wake her up for the final seconds of the year or enjoy resting beside her. Genevieve fell asleep.

Genevieve didn't wake up until close to one in the

morning. First, she opened her right eye and surveyed her dark living room. Genevieve opened her other eye and struggled to focus, but when her vision cleared, she had a lot to take in.

Harper was stretched out on her back along the couch, pressed against the cushions. Genevieve was also lying down fully, but she was on her side, one leg over Harper's. Genevieve could smell Harper's laundry detergent from the shirt her face was buried in. Genevieve's hand rested on Harper's abdomen, just at the hem of her thermal. Her pinkie danced along the fine line between soft material and bare skin. Genevieve wanted to feel Harper's skin and decided to lift her shirt and place her hand flat against the sleeping woman's stomach. Harper's abdomen was all taut muscle and soft skin, and Genevieve's breathing grew shallow. She didn't move her hand or her body, and she closed her eyes to lose herself to everything around her.

Harper stirred, but Genevieve continued to fake her slumber. Harper put her hand over Genevieve's wandering one and held it briefly. Genevieve felt momentarily ashamed, as if she had crossed a line, but Harper didn't move her hand. Instead, Harper pressed her lips to Genevieve's forehead and whispered her a Happy New Year.

Genevieve moved slowly, feigning the sluggishness that accompanies awaking unexpectedly. She looked up at Harper, batting her eyelashes as if they were coated in molasses, and smiled brightly. "You're comfy." She pulled her hand away and rubbed at her eyes.

"How long have we been out for?"

"A little over an hour, I think." Genevieve sat up and Harper followed, stretching out her long limbs. "You missed the end of the movie."

"We missed the ball drop."

Genevieve felt a flash of guilt for not waking her, but she

wanted this moment, not an awkward countdown and inevitable "should we or shouldn't we" as they watched couples on TV kiss. This intimacy was so much more rewarding than anything forced. Their first kiss had been in response to a stupid holiday tradition, and Genevieve didn't want their second to be the same.

Harper stood. "I should get going."

"You can stay if you'd like." Genevieve nearly jumped from the couch and rushed to Harper's side as she pulled on her boots. Harper gave her a slow, sleepy smile that brought back every rapid heartbeat Genevieve felt when she placed her palm against Harper's bare skin. "I can sleep out here."

"I don't live far from here. Besides, I don't have a change of clothes." Harper shrugged on her coat and stood within inches of Genevieve. She brought her hand up to Genevieve's jaw and cradled her face gently. "If I'm spending the night, I'm going to do it right."

"I'll keep that in mind," Genevieve said. Before she could say more, Harper ran her thumb along her full bottom lip.

Genevieve's knees started to give out. Every time Harper touched her, her body responded with more intensity than it would to a directly stimulated erogenous zone. Genevieve puckered her lips and kissed Harper's fingertip.

"Harper, kiss me. Please."

Harper kissed her so firmly Genevieve had to grip the front of Harper's jacket to remain standing. They had no audience this time. Genevieve kissed Harper's upper lip, and then the lower. Harper combed her fingers through the fine hairs that danced along Genevieve's neck while she kissed her back gently. Harper traced the bow of Genevieve's upper lip with the tip of her tongue and Genevieve moaned quietly, her throat tight with growing desire.

Genevieve felt along Harper's upper chest and shoulders

for anything to keep her steady, grazing Harper's breast through her winter jacket. The touch wasn't intentional or firm, but Harper's breath caught, and she cradled the back of Genevieve's head as she kissed her more forcefully.

Genevieve backed up slowly, remaining connected to Harper as she found purchase against the edge of her sofa. She pulled back from the kiss to take a few necessary deep breaths, and Harper kissed her neck. Moving her hands away from Genevieve's disheveled hair, Harper's fingertips danced along the column of her neck down to the collar of her shirt, tugging it open and nipping at Genevieve's collarbone.

"Harper," Genevieve whimpered. She spread her legs as she leaned back onto the couch, hoping Harper would give her just a little pressure where she throbbed between her thighs, but Harper stood her ground and kept the assault centered on Genevieve's sensitive neck and upper chest. Genevieve squirmed against the back of the couch, trying to guide Harper's attention lower and lower, knowing Harper's hands would be on her breasts at any moment. But she misjudged her balance and tumbled to the floor with a yelp.

"You can laugh," Genevieve said, wide-eyed on the floor, breathing heavily against the hand that had saved her face from impact with the carpet.

Harper giggled, gripping her sides and encouraging her up. When she was standing, Genevieve finally took a good look at Harper and the effect she'd had on her. Harper was noticeably flushed, even in the dark room, and her normally impeccable hair was mussed.

"I'm sorry," Genevieve said out of habit.

"For what?" Harper looked genuinely confused. "I had a great time tonight, and I think this was the perfect start to the New Year." Harper leaned in and kissed Genevieve's cheek sweetly. "But I really must go now, otherwise I'll never leave." Harper zipped her jacket closed.

"You say that like it's a bad thing," Genevieve said with raised eyebrows. Harper didn't answer, but she shot Genevieve a mischievous smirk. They walked together to the door and Genevieve reluctantly watched as Harper started down the hallway toward the stairs.

"Drive safe!" she called out in a loud whisper, conscious of any sleeping neighbors. Harper looked back to her and winked, and then she was gone.

Genevieve closed her apartment door and walked straight to the bathroom. As tired as she was, she was immensely turned on, and a shower would either calm her down or she'd spend some quality alone time with her right hand. Judging by the dampened state of her underwear, the latter was much more likely.

STEP EIGHTEEN

Don't Let Others Discourage You

Genevieve had filled Chloe in on what had happened with Jeremy and the latest developments with Harper. She spared no details and didn't care if she sounded sickening. For once, she was happy with every aspect of her life, and she finally felt like she belonged.

She was back at work two days later, in the office for less than two hours before she polished her latest piece and sent it off to Harper, who she had yet to see that day. Since their impromptu New Year's Eve, Genevieve and Harper had exchanged countless texts but hadn't had a real conversation. They'd flirt, make references to their evening together, and even discuss the possibility of going on a date, but nothing had come of it. Genevieve was getting antsy, but she didn't let that affect her work. She typed and typed, getting a jump start on the next week's installment, figuring she'd be able to free up her social calendar if she finished it early.

Genevieve had a sandwich at her desk for lunch so she could keep her focus and forward momentum, but that was broken by the sound of whistling. When she turned around, Harper was waving off the attention of the staff as she approached Genevieve's desk.

"Remind me to never kiss you in front of an audience again," Harper said, much to the delight of Maxine who started laughing. "Genevieve, may I see you in my office for a minute?" She looked pointedly at Maxine. "For *business*."

"Sure." Genevieve removed her glasses and stood sheepishly. Once they were behind the closed door, however, Genevieve pushed Harper gently, guiding her to sit on the edge of her desk as she positioned herself between Harper's spread legs. "You wanted to see me, *boss*?" she said in a playfully sweet voice as she toyed with the buttons of Harper's gray dress shirt.

"I did." Harper cleared her throat, obviously surprised by this turn of events. "I missed you."

Genevieve softened. "You did?" She stepped back, only to be drawn back into Harper's arms.

"I did, and I really wanted to do this..." Harper pulled Genevieve in for a soft kiss that quickly escalated into roaming hands and heavy breathing. Genevieve pulled away first, worrying someone would burst through the door with a magazine emergency. "Don't worry about that. Dana knows no one comes in if my door is closed."

"You do this often?" Genevieve was mostly joking, but her apprehension must've shone through her smile because Harper looked her in the eye when she replied.

"I spend a lot of time alone in here, thinking and planning and taking way too many serious phone calls. But this?" She grabbed Genevieve's hands and held them to her chest. "This is the first time in a long while I'm abusing my privilege."

Even with Harper's most charming smile shining at her, Genevieve's heart sank slightly when she realized that "first time in a long while" meant this wasn't the first time ever. She brushed off these negative thoughts and sank deeper into Harper's embrace. Genevieve leaned forward and kissed Harper again.

"I could get used to this," Genevieve mumbled against Harper's lips.

"Me too, but we should really try to remain professional." Harper's actions contradicted her words as she reached down and cupped Genevieve's backside through her tight pencil skirt. Genevieve stifled a moan.

"If you keep that up," Genevieve said in between kisses, "I'm going to go way beyond professional."

Harper pulled back from Genevieve and put her hands up where Genevieve could see them. "As tempting as that is, I'm more romantic than that."

Genevieve straightened herself up. "I had a feeling you would be."

"Oh? What other feelings did you have about me?"

Genevieve smiled and toyed with Harper's collar as she spoke. "I had a feeling you'd be kind and romantic, and I knew you'd be a great kisser. I also have a feeling that you're great at many other things." Genevieve wasn't sure if she was being affected by Harper or by being at work, but she never wanted to stop teasing her.

"Come to dinner with me tonight."

Genevieve cocked her head at the invitation. "Another business dinner?" She poked at Harper's hard stomach.

"No business, all pleasure," Harper said in nearly a purr.

Genevieve felt a delightful pull in her lower abdomen. "Pick me up?"

"Seven o'clock."

Genevieve gave Harper a chaste kiss before she left the office. During the short walk back to her desk, Genevieve touched her lips lightly and daydreamed of how kissing Harper was so much better than anything she had experienced in the past. Genevieve was so dazed with thoughts of the night to come, she didn't see Clarissa in front of her until they collided.

"You should really watch where you're going," Clarissa said. "Or else someone may get hurt."

"Sorry." Genevieve turned away.

"Listen, Gen, I don't know what game you're playing, but you need to put an end to it."

"I don't know what you're talking about."

"Those big blue eyes may work on Harper, but not me. I know exactly what you're up to, Genevieve Applegate from Milan, Pennsylvania. Google is an amazing thing, you know?" Clarissa started to circle Genevieve where she stood, like a shark smelling blood in the water. "I found out some interesting things about you, and I'll be glad to share it all with Harper."

"Please, Clarissa, it's not what it looks like. It started out as a small lie—"

"A small lie?" She laughed. "Lying about your sexual orientation in a place like this is a big deal." Genevieve looked around in a panic, hoping no one would overhear them. "And if you didn't agree, then you wouldn't look so worried right now."

"I'm going to tell her."

"Yes, you are, or I'm going to, because she doesn't deserve to be lied to," Clarissa said as she walked away.

Genevieve stood shaken. The lies that had gotten her this far no longer felt like lies. She thought of them as delayed truth, but that didn't sound much better. Genevieve hoped Harper would understand her rationale.

It looked like date night was going to become confession night.

Step Nineteen

Listen to What Your Body's Telling You

Genevieve was very familiar with nervousness. She'd even feel safe saying she had thrived on it at one time, whether it was pre-performance jitters before a grade school talent competition or standing in the middle of a basketball court in sixth grade to prove she wasn't entirely incompetent at sports. But this time, Genevieve's nerves made her nauseous, which hopefully wouldn't lead to inappropriate vomiting.

She took a deep breath and released it shakily as she looked herself over in her bedroom mirror. She had bought a dress on her way home just for the occasion. A date, a *real* date with Harper deserved something new, so when Genevieve had come across the burgundy knee-length dress at a local shop, she cared very little about the price. Genevieve felt beautiful in it. With her hair down and straightened, Genevieve looked like she was ready for a hot date, but she knew tonight wouldn't be that simple.

This date would have to be about coming clean and admitting to months of lies. Better Harper hear it from her than Clarissa. Genevieve had to be prepared to tell it all and sell Harper on all the positives that came from one momentary lapse in judgment.

"Everything happens for a reason, right?" Genevieve grimaced at her reflection. She felt more like an inmate on death row rather than a woman getting ready for a date with someone she was crazy about. She checked the time again. Harper was running ten minutes late. Her heart started beating harder.

Maybe Clarissa had spoken to Harper first. That wouldn't surprise Genevieve in the slightest. Or maybe Harper had discovered the truth on her own. Like Clarissa said, Google was a wonderful tool. Genevieve's blood pressure rose. Who was Clarissa to meddle like this? Why did she care so much about making Genevieve's life a living hell?

The doorbell rang, and Genevieve clamped her eyes shut. *You can do this,* Genevieve thought as she walked to the door. *Tell the truth and point out all the good that has happened since you started at the magazine.* Genevieve opened the door to see Harper shuffling nervously on the other side. Her heart swelled at the sight. When Harper looked up at her with bashful gray eyes, Genevieve struggled to keep her rationale at the forefront of her mind and push her admiration and desire to the back.

Harper broke the silence by apologizing for her tardiness. "I wanted to get you flowers," she said. "But I couldn't find any place local that had anything nice and alive, so I got you these instead." Harper pulled a white plastic bag from behind her back and handed it to Genevieve, who looked inside eagerly.

"Gummy bears?"

"A dozen bags of gummy bears, to be precise," Harper said proudly. "I know they're your favorite."

"Oh they are, thank you." Genevieve stepped closer to Harper, not just to show her appreciation, but to relish their closeness in case it all disappeared. She silently cursed the thickness of Harper's winter jacket because she couldn't feel the strong body beneath it.

Harper kissed Genevieve's cheek briefly and stepped back. "We have a reservation to get to in eighteen minutes. Grab your coat and let's go. You can bring the candy just in case there's nothing on the menu you'll enjoy as much."

Genevieve rolled her eyes and laughed. "I can find something to eat anywhere," she said as she gathered her things.

"We're actually going for pizza."

"Pizza?" Genevieve said. She stood outside Harper's car and eyed her. Judging by the smirk on Harper's full lips, Genevieve thought they were in for much more than pizza.

❖

The small, gourmet pizzeria boasted words such as *organic* and *vegan*, with cheeses far from the overprocessed white stuff Genevieve was used to seeing piled on top of a pizza. She'd never seen salad for a topping, or people eating pizza with a knife and fork.

"Not what you were expecting?" said Harper.

"You said pizza."

"It is pizza, just *fancy* pizza."

"Hence the outfit?" Genevieve pointed to Harper's gray and white checkered button-up and perfectly pressed charcoal dress pants.

"I would've dressed up no matter what. I want to impress you."

Genevieve blushed. "You don't have to do that, Harper."

"Says a girl who has obviously never been impressed." Harper looked at Genevieve intently across their small table, the light coming from a series of small votive candles illuminating her face warmly. "You look stunning, by the way."

"You're not the only one looking to impress someone tonight, though I'm sure I'm not the first woman to ever impress you," Genevieve said with a raised eyebrow before sipping at her water.

"You're right, but you're the first woman who's managed to impress me every day. And I'm not just talking about your looks."

Genevieve looked away from Harper, trying hard to keep any guilt from showing in her face. "Harper, I'm not impressive."

"Yes you are. Genevieve, you came here from essentially the middle of nowhere to pursue a career—a dream, really—and you're excelling at it. You should be proud of yourself. You've changed your life in a way so many people wish they could."

Genevieve felt many emotions at the moment, but pride definitely wasn't one of them. "You order," she said as the waiter approached. "I have no idea what to get." Genevieve was grateful for Harper's take-charge attitude because it bought her time to arrange her scattered thoughts.

Once their orders were placed, they talked about the magazine and the restaurant until their food arrived and their conversation dwindled away to silence.

"Now, this is a perfect first date spot," Genevieve said as they ate.

"I was hoping you'd say that. I remember you imagining what is was like to be on a date with me. Am I living up to imaginary Harper?"

"The real thing is so much better." Genevieve licked a small spot of sauce from her thumb and slid her plate to the side. It was time. "I wanted to talk to you about something."

"Wait." Harper put down her napkin and cleared her throat. "There's something I need to get out before you say anything more." She took a deep breath. "I was putting it off, avoiding it because I didn't want to ruin our night, but if I don't talk about it, I'll hate myself." Genevieve started to panic. "We need to talk about Clarissa."

Genevieve's stomach dropped. She knew dinner was a bad idea. Who eats before willingly throwing themselves into an emotional confrontation? She nearly choked on the rolling of her stomach. "Has she said something to you?"

"It's what she's been saying to you, or not saying. Or doing." Harper struggled momentarily. "This is about how she's been treating you."

"Like I said, she's a bully. You said it yourself. She doesn't like the attention you give me."

"It's a bit more complicated than that." Harper wiped her hands against her legs, more nervous than Genevieve had ever seen her.

"Harper?"

When Harper spoke again, it was directly to her empty dinner plate. "Clarissa is my ex-wife."

"I'm sorry, I didn't hear you. I thought you said she's your ex-wife." Harper didn't repeat herself or even look at Genevieve. "Harper, is Clarissa your ex-wife?"

Harper only nodded.

"The ex-wife that cheated on you? Please talk!" People at the tables around her gave Genevieve a dirty look. She was embarrassed, but much more concerned with Harper.

"Clarissa is my ex-wife, the one who cheated on me while we were still newlyweds, yes."

"Then why the *hell* does she work for you?" Genevieve tried to keep her voice even and low, but the words came out like a growl.

Harper looked at Genevieve pleadingly. "Because she wasn't the same Clarissa back then. We were together for a reason—she was kind and funny, and she wanted the best for both of us. She helped me get the magazine up and running after my uncle passed. He ran a small publication, but what I had in mind was so much bigger than that, and it was bigger than me. She believed in me." Harper placed her hand on the tabletop. Genevieve resisted the strong urge she felt to cover it with her own. "I needed help, and she knew the right people. Between her connections and the popularity of her column, we were succeeding."

"Do you feel like you owe her something?"

"No, not anymore, but her articles were some of the most popular until yours." Harper smirked at Genevieve. Harper turned her hand over and waited until Genevieve placed her hand in Harper's. "Genevieve, you are the first woman I've been interested in since the divorce. Clarissa can sense that. That's the reason why she's been so horrible toward you."

"That, and how I threaten her popularity amongst readers."

"That too, for sure."

"Do you think she still has feelings for you?"

Harper shook her head. "She still cares, just like I'll always care about her, but it's no longer love."

"Isn't it weird having your ex around all the time?"

"Not really. A lot of lesbians have the tendency to stay friends with their exes. I'm guilty of it, and I don't even understand it."

"Friends?"

"Work acquaintances," Harper said. "I know this is a lot to take in, and I'll respect any decision you make."

"Decision?"

"If you need time and space or whatever. Just tell me,

Genevieve. It'll suck, but I want to move past this and still have a chance with you."

Genevieve gripped Harper's hand tighter. "I need the opposite, actually. I want to be closer to you. The hardest part to accept is the Clarissa you know and the Clarissa I know being the same person."

Harper laughed. "Our time together changed us both, and I think she's afraid of ending up in the same position again. Like I was, until you."

Genevieve felt herself getting lost in Harper's loving gaze. She needed to say her piece now. She took a deep breath. "I need to tell you something, too, but this isn't the place."

Harper beckoned for their waiter and paid their check quickly. She ushered Genevieve out to the car, never once relinquishing contact, whether it was softly gripping Genevieve's elbow or wrapping her arm around her waist. The small, chivalrous gesture was a new experience for Genevieve. Jeremy had never done that for her. They were two kids who had grown into a relationship, bypassing the little things that made romance and love all the sweeter. Most of the time he'd even walk ahead of her whenever they were together.

Harper opened her car door for her, made sure she was settled with her seat belt on before pulling into traffic, and most importantly, she held Genevieve's hand the entire silent ride back to her apartment. Once they were inside, Genevieve walked directly to her refrigerator.

"Beer?"

"No, thank you." Harper stripped off her coat and sat back on Genevieve's couch.

Genevieve felt guilty for drinking while Harper remained sober, so she didn't drink her beer, but she kept it in case she needed to drown her sorrows at the end of her confession.

Harper had taken off her shoes, lounging casually and comfortably on the sofa.

"Are you okay?" Harper said.

"Fine, yeah, sorry." She shook off her stupor and sat beside Harper. "I was just thinking of the last time you were here."

"I haven't stopped thinking about that night. All I've wanted since this afternoon was to kiss you again." Harper started to lean in.

Genevieve pulled back and blurted, "I've never been with a woman."

Harper looked at Genevieve with kind, understanding eyes. "I'm not going to rush you."

"No, it's not that. This is what I've been trying to tell you." Genevieve took a deep breath, trying to steady herself as her anxiety made her dizzy. "I've never been with a woman, in a relationship or otherwise." She struggled to get the exact words out.

"Genevieve," Harper said, taking Genevieve's hands and pulling them into her lap. "I don't care. Everyone grows at their own pace, and considering where you came from, it doesn't surprise me you weren't able to live fully as a single woman."

"There's not much when it comes to gay living in Milan."

"The past is the past. You're not judging me on mine, why should I judge you on yours? Hell, I don't even care if your last relationship was Jeremy!" Genevieve swallowed roughly. "All I care about is this moment and how I feel about you."

Genevieve stared at Harper dreamily. "How *do* you feel about me?"

Harper flashed a small smile. "You're a breath of fresh air for me. I knew the moment you walked into your interview that I needed to get to know you better. And not just because of the sweat stains," she deadpanned.

Genevieve laughed unabashedly and covered her face. Harper pulled her hands away and said, "You always do that. Don't hide from me." Genevieve continued to watch Harper with awe. "I've managed to go so many years without falling for someone, claiming self-preservation or something. But I'm starting to think I was just waiting for you." Harper reached out and brushed a few strands of Genevieve's hair from her face. She ran the pad of thumb along her cheek and down to trace her lips.

"Harper..." Genevieve said breathily.

"I'm ready to court you." Harper laughed at Genevieve's giggle. "I'm following your lead. You set the pace for our future—whatever you're comfortable with."

Regardless of the promise she made to herself to be more introspective and critical of decisions when it came to Harper, Genevieve didn't have to think very long before she knew exactly what she wanted next. "Take me to bed, Harper."

STEP TWENTY

Indulge in What Makes You Feel Good

Genevieve's cheeks flushed. *Take me to bed? Did I really just say that? No one says that except women in their fifties who are ready to take their pool boy for a spin.*

"Genevieve?"

She snapped back to the moment and looked to an expectant Harper.

"Are you sure?"

She could tell Harper how ready she was until she was blue in the face, and Harper would still remain hesitant because she cared for Genevieve's comfort first and foremost. Harper was very sweet, but Genevieve was ready to move beyond sweet and into something spicy. So instead of answering Harper, Genevieve acted instead.

Genevieve gripped Harper's collar and tugged on it, bringing her in for a kiss. She kissed Harper firmly, gliding her lips against Harper's before tasting Harper's mouth with the tip of her tongue. Harper moaned softly. That sound, mixed with the scent of Harper's body so close, spurred Genevieve on. She continued to pull at Harper's clothes and intensified her kiss, losing herself in the addictiveness of Harper's velvety tongue dancing along with hers. Pulling and pulling, Genevieve tried to lie down, but Harper pulled back.

Harper looked at Genevieve with pure adoration. "You asked me to take you to bed, Ms. Applegate. This is the sofa."

"I don't care if it's the floor at this point."

"Come on." Harper stood and lifted Genevieve into her arms. Genevieve squealed in surprise.

"You're strong."

"You're small." Within a few short steps, she set Genevieve onto her feet and looked into her smiling face. "What would you like?"

Genevieve thought through various ways to answer, shifting between dirty and honest or innocent and honest. She decided on a balance of both. "All of you." She reached up and placed her palm against Harper's cheek. "I want all of you, *now*."

"My pleasure."

When Harper kissed Genevieve again, a noticeable shift had taken place between them. Harper had become more firm without losing her natural gentleness that made Genevieve feel revered. But Harper's passion was now being let off its leash, and she dug her fingertips into Genevieve's hips with painful, unrestrained pleasure.

They were locked in an embrace at the foot of Genevieve's bed, and Genevieve was dizzy at the multitude of sensations. Harper trailed soft kisses along her jaw, spending a few moments below Genevieve's earlobe before she turned her attention to Genevieve's sensitive neck.

"You smell so good," Harper mumbled against Genevieve's neck. Goose bumps spread across her flesh. Genevieve stared blankly at her ceiling and focused on Harper's hands traveling along her back and down to grip her ass. "You feel even better," Harper whispered into Genevieve's ear. Genevieve ran her fingers into the short hairs at the nape of Harper's neck, giving them a gentle tug.

Genevieve sat on her mattress and looked up to Harper through hooded eyelids.

"Do you have any idea how long I've wanted this?" Harper said.

"If how I feel right now is any indication, I'm willing to guess far too long."

Harper smirked salaciously. Without breaking eye contact, she unbuttoned her shirt.

Genevieve sat transfixed. She wanted to help Harper. Hell, she wanted to push Harper's hands away and take charge of getting this gorgeous woman naked, but she was frozen with desire. Being a voyeur was just as wonderful as being a participant. Harper opened her shirt to reveal a crisp, white undershirt she quickly shed.

Her imagination did Harper's body little justice. She was the perfect combination of definition and tone. Genevieve was hypnotized by the few inches between her navel and the waistband of her pants. She stared, marveling at how incredibly soft the skin looked. She was overwhelmed with the urge to drag her short nails across it, taste it with the tip of her tongue, and mark it as explored territory. Genevieve looked up at the flame dancing in Harper's gaze.

"How are you so sexy? Are you even real?" Genevieve wondered aloud.

Harper chuckled, stripping off her belt and dropping her pants to the floor. Harper's hard nipples were visible through her black sports bra, and her short boxer briefs hugged her muscular thighs.

"Seriously unreal."

Harper stepped forward, bringing her perky breasts closer to Genevieve. Genevieve closed her eyes at the feel of Harper's fingers weaving into her long hair. When she tilted her head back, Harper rewarded her with a sweet kiss on her parted lips.

Harper's hands fell to Genevieve's thighs, her fingertips just beneath the hem of her dress, moving upward slowly. She looked at Genevieve and said, "I'm feeling a little underdressed right now."

"Fix that, then," Genevieve demanded, canting her hips slightly to encourage Harper. She knew just how well Harper took charge in the office; now she wanted to see that in the bedroom.

Harper responded quickly, pushing roughly at Genevieve's skirt until the material was bunched around her hips. Harper's palms never lost contact with Genevieve's bare skin. With a firm grip on Genevieve's buttocks, Harper pulled Genevieve to the edge of the mattress.

"Can this go over your head?" Harper said, and Genevieve took it off completely. She looked down at Genevieve's body and said, "Now who's unreal and sexy?"

Genevieve blushed and mentally high-fived herself for picking out a lacy matching set of lingerie in hopes of Harper getting to see it.

Harper knelt in front of the mattress. "I want you, Genevieve, but I'm serious when I say I don't want to rush you. If you don't feel comfortable at any time, tell me. Okay?"

Genevieve nodded.

"Now," Harper said, running the fingertips of her right hand along Genevieve's collarbone and down her sternum. "I think the best way to make sure you're comfortable is to communicate clearly." Harper brushed her left hand across Genevieve's thighs.

Genevieve's reply came in a shaky, breathy moan. "Okay." She spread her legs, and Harper moved closer, showering Genevieve's chest with kisses.

"Are you comfortable with this?" Harper said, as she grazed her lips along the top of Genevieve's bra.

Genevieve felt her nipples constrict, as if trying to answer Harper themselves. "Yes," she nearly hissed. She wanted to pull it off, but she didn't. She could barely move once Harper's hands began traveling her bare abdomen.

"Are you comfortable if I touch you here?" Harper dipped her fingertip into Genevieve's navel before she spread both hands across her thighs. "And here?"

"I'm comfortable," Genevieve said in a strangled voice. "But I'd be even more comfortable if you took this bra off me."

Harper winked and did as Genevieve demanded.

The cool air hit Genevieve's bare breasts, and she shivered from both the chill and the exposure. Harper stared, and Genevieve began to shrink away from her intense gaze, but she saw a glimmer of awe sparkling there.

"You're stunning," Harper said.

Genevieve giggled. "Are you talking to me or my tits?"

Harper kissed her passionately. "You *and* your tits," she said when she pulled back. She took a waiting nipple into her mouth, paying the pebbled flesh the perfect amount of attention, biting and licking. Once Genevieve started to squirm, pulling at the hair on the back of Harper's head, Harper ascended her abdomen. She placed kisses on her trembling flesh, Genevieve's muscles contracting each time Harper's lips landed on previously untouched skin. With each kiss she felt weaker, and when Harper sank her teeth into her hip bone, Genevieve fell back against the bed.

"Are you comfortable?" Harper said.

Genevieve hummed her response, not able to form coherent words while she focused on the warmth of Harper's breath against her inner thighs. Her skin was on fire. She could feel her blood rushing throughout her limbs, and she was hypersensitive to every stimulant around her. Harper branded her skin with her lips and hands. The scent of Genevieve's own desire filled her nose. Genevieve could still taste Harper's lips on hers. And when Genevieve looked down, Harper's hungry eyes stared back.

"I'm going to remove these now." She hooked her thumbs into the band of Genevieve's panties. "Is that okay?"

Genevieve raised her hips in response.

She was briefly struck with self-consciousness, thinking she should be ashamed of the way she reacted to Harper's touch. She started to close her legs, to hide her copious arousal from Harper, but Harper persuaded her knees apart, and Genevieve gave in willingly at the sight of Harper licking her lips. For the first time in her life, she felt like a sexy woman.

In a bold move, she let her head fall to the mattress and bowed her back, thrusting her naked chest up. "Please," she whispered.

The instant Harper's tongue made contact with Genevieve's pulsing flesh, Genevieve clamped her eyes shut. The world went black to everything except Harper's tongue caressing her most intimate places. Genevieve keened at Harper's enthusiastic exploration of her every saturated fold. She moved her hips in time, around and around to ensure that not even a millimeter went untouched.

Each slick pass of Harper's tongue drove Genevieve higher toward a peak of pleasure, and when Harper centered her attention on her swollen clit, she was sure no better feeling existed. As she writhed in passion, Harper slowed her attention. When Genevieve looked down, Harper was grinning at her wickedly. Genevieve didn't have much time to wonder what Harper was up to before she felt the tip of Harper's finger tease her fluttering entrance.

"Are you—"

"Yesss…" Genevieve lay back once again, ready for the pleasure to take over.

Harper entered her slowly, much to Genevieve's delight. She was able to focus on every sensation that overwhelmed her as Harper passed another knuckle through her tight opening. She felt spasms begin.

"Another, please, I'm so close," Genevieve begged in a high voice. Harper obliged and Genevieve could've sworn she saw stars the moment Harper slid two fingers into her with unexpected force. Genevieve moved her hips again, chasing her impending orgasm by riding Harper's fingers and grinding against her tongue.

"You're so sexy," Harper whispered, as Genevieve reached up and pinched her own nipples. Harper's breath quickened, and Genevieve wondered what effect she was having on her.

The thought that she was turning Harper on, reducing the professional woman to a quivering mess, drove Genevieve to the edge, and her orgasm took over. She came loudly, the breath leaving her lungs in a whoosh as every sensation that started in her toes, belly, and heart gathered directly between her legs.

"Harper!" Genevieve called out as she threaded her fingers into Harper's hair, holding her mouth in place against her skin as she rode out the final waves of pleasure. She didn't release her hold until she became too sensitive for even the lightest touch and had to push Harper's head away.

Something in Genevieve broke the moment Harper stood and looked down at her. It could've been the softness in her eyes or the pride in her smile, but a dam burst in Genevieve and she started to cry.

"Hey," Harper cooed. She climbed on the bed and cradled

Genevieve in her arms, bringing her to lie in the center of the bed. "You're okay. I've got you."

They lay together for a long while as Genevieve cried softly, lost in the swell of emotion. Harper ran her fingers through her hair and lavished Genevieve's brows and temples with featherlight kisses. Genevieve knew exactly why she was crying. She was relieved and in love.

Step Twenty-one

Accept Your New Role

After Genevieve's cries had subsided, Harper continued to hold her close and soothe her with gentle caresses. Genevieve lay with her head on her hand, facing Harper and smiling softly.

"When did you know you were gay?" Genevieve said. "I know about Trevor, but when did you really know and accept it?"

"I suppose I always knew, but things started to make sense around senior year when things were off again with Trevor because spending time with my best *girlfriend* was more important to me. I started to realize it wasn't about Trevor or my friend, it was about me."

"I bet you were adorable."

Harper laughed. "I was awkward and gangly and impossibly shy."

"When did you blossom into this gorgeous human being?" Genevieve said, putting her index finger at the center of Harper's chin.

"My late twenties, when I learned the importance of a good haircut and having a tailor."

"The second thing I noticed about you was how well your clothes fit."

"What was the first?"

"Your eyes." Genevieve said. She traced the lines of Harper's brows and along the bridge of her nose. "They're amazing. I was lost the moment you looked at me."

"And the moment I looked at you, I thought you were the most beautiful woman that had ever sat across from me."

"Oh, please."

"I mean it, Genevieve."

"Thank you, really, but I just find that hard to believe."

"Why?" Harper said, a hint of hurt in her voice.

Genevieve paused, but she had promised herself she'd be honest with Harper from now on. She took a deep breath and said, "You were married to Clarissa."

"And you're more beautiful than she ever was or will be to me. Inside and out."

Genevieve took in Harper's dreamy eyes and messed hair. She leaned forward and kissed her, alternating between firm exploratory kisses and shallow kisses. Harper caressed Genevieve's body, her hips starting to move involuntarily. Harper's breaths grew more rapid, Genevieve pulled back and looked her in the eye. "I want to touch you."

"And I won't stop you. But I don't want you to feel like you have to."

"I *need* to." Genevieve scraped her short fingernails over Harper's covered nipples. "Take this off first." Harper did as told, removing her underwear as well before resuming her position in bed.

Genevieve was about to admit she didn't know what she was doing, but she realized she was more excited to discover what made Harper feel good than she was worried about being an inexperienced mess. She planned on taking her time in learning her body well, and she didn't hesitate to get started.

Genevieve felt along Harper's shoulders, reveling in the firm muscles that flexed beneath the soft skin. She counted each freckle along the way as she trailed her fingertips down to Harper's breasts. Genevieve took her first long look at Harper's naked body. She was surprised by how much darker her nipples were, and Harper's breasts were bigger than she expected. Genevieve reached out to fill her hand with one and nearly jumped when Harper shivered.

Harper blushed. "It's been a while. I forgot how sensitive I am."

Genevieve caressed Harper's breast again and pinched her nipple. Harper's squeal changed to a throaty moan, a noise Genevieve wanted to hear again and again. She pushed Harper back and straddled her thighs. Harper's mouth fell open. Genevieve explored Harper's torso with her lips, leaving moist ringlets in the wake of open-mouthed kisses. She lavished attention on Harper's chest, nipping and licking at her skin before taking one pert nipple between her lips.

Harper moaned again. Genevieve redoubled her efforts, swirling her tongue around the dusky peak as she scraped it gently between her teeth. Harper had started to move her hips, grabbing on to Genevieve's hips with a near-painful hold and throwing her head back into the pillow. Genevieve read the peaks and valleys of Harper's abs with her fingertips, as if painting a picture in her memory. She reached below Harper's navel, where she traced the two sexy muscles that formed a V. Genevieve wanted to look into Harper's eyes once more, but they were closed.

Her face flushed, Harper appeared lost in an immense pleasure Genevieve was responsible for and in control of. When Genevieve reached down between Harper's legs, she gasped at how wet she was.

"Don't be so surprised," Harper said without even looking at Genevieve. Her voice was raspy and strained as she spoke. "I haven't calmed down since I started touching you."

Genevieve ran her middle finger down to her entrance, the source of her flowing desire. She nearly growled in response. Genevieve could feel Harper's heart pounding from the inside out, syncing with her own thundering heartbeat. She explored Harper's depths, humming in approval when she skimmed along her thick, achingly pronounced clit.

"Someone's excited."

"You have no idea," Harper said between clenched teeth.

"Oh I have an idea." Genevieve sat up and situated herself with one of Harper's legs between hers. She ground down on Harper's muscular thigh, spreading her wetness across her skin. Harper's breathing stuttered to a halt, and she released a long breath once Genevieve continued the movement between her legs.

Genevieve pressed firmly against Harper's clit, circling the turgid bud with three fingers. Genevieve's hand moved smoothly in her juices, and she never stopped moving her hips as she rode Harper's leg. She was chasing pleasure as well as giving, and the power in that turned Genevieve on even more.

"I'm close again," she said.

"Me too."

Genevieve moved her hand faster, willing Harper to find the same bliss she was about to embark upon. Her own orgasm took her by surprise. She had no lengthy buildup, just a solitary explosion between her legs against Harper's heated flesh. Genevieve fell forward against Harper and struggled to keep her movement even for the sake of the writhing woman beneath her. In a final effort to share in ecstasy together, Genevieve bit down on Harper's breast.

"Genevieve," Harper panted. "Don't stop!"

Harper dug her fingers into Genevieve's skin, and Genevieve hoped she'd be forever branded with her touch. Memories weren't enough, not for this moment. She needed a natural tattoo to follow her until her dying day.

Harper came silently, ceasing all movement as her body locked. Genevieve continued to caress her as she rode out every spasm. When Harper stopped moving, Genevieve looked down into her peaceful face and knew she had found exactly where her heart belonged.

❖

"What a way to wake up," Genevieve mumbled sleepily, feeling bare, warm skin pressed against hers. Harper glided her hands along Genevieve's thighs and stomach. Genevieve wanted to forget alarm clocks for the rest of her life and be awakened like this.

Harper pressed a soft kiss against Genevieve's bare shoulder. "I didn't mean to wake you. I just needed to feel you to make sure this was real and not some incredible dream. How are you?"

Genevieve smiled at Harper's concern. She wondered whether Harper was always so considerate and caring. She faced Harper. "I'm wonderful," she said softly, placing her palm against Harper's cheek. "And I'll be even better once I brush my teeth."

They both giggled before Genevieve leapt from the bed and ran to the bathroom naked. She stood back from the large mirror over the sink and looked at her reflection, her cheeks rosy and her smile blinding. Her eyes were a little red from her unexpected tears but were shimmering and clear otherwise. She felt a twinge of embarrassment when she saw her old makeup and mussed hair. Genevieve washed her face quickly and struggled to recognize herself on the outside. The woman she was back in Pennsylvania was no more. Now Genevieve Applegate was the person she believed she could be all along— accomplished, independent, and desirable.

"Harper?" she called out over her shoulder. "I have an extra toothbrush."

Within seconds Harper was next to her, tearing open the plastic packaging.

"Eager?" Genevieve said.

"I want my lips on you, and I'm also a firm believer in superior dental hygiene."

"It shows. Your smile is gorgeous." Genevieve looked at Harper naked in the morning sunlight. This was the first unobstructed glimpse she'd had, and Genevieve took full advantage of the opportunity. Harper's hair was mussed, the complete opposite of its everyday perfection. Genevieve loved it. "Just like the rest of you," she said.

"Stop with the compliments. They're going to inflate my ego, and no one wants a conceited girlfriend." Harper bent over the sink and started to brush her teeth. Genevieve laughed before Harper's words fully registered in her head. She brushed her teeth slowly, making the same small circles over and over until Harper smiled brilliantly at Genevieve in the mirror and said, "Ready for more kissing."

Genevieve spat out the excess toothpaste as delicately as possible and wiped her mouth with a dampened hand towel. She finished quickly, wrapping her arms around Harper's neck and pressing their bodies together. Harper took a sharp breath. Genevieve kissed her softly, enjoying the minty taste. "Are you my girlfriend?" She tried to pull back to look into Harper's eyes, but Harper didn't let her. She intensified the kiss.

She pulled back, leaving Genevieve panting, and said, "I'm kissing you in your bathroom, completely naked after brushing our teeth together. I think that puts us at girlfriend status. What do you think?"

"I agree, but I think there needs to be more kissing before I know for sure."

Genevieve squealed when Harper lifted her up and carried her to bed.

Much later, when the couple became too hungry to stay in bed, they dragged themselves to the kitchen for a hearty brunch of cold cereal. Harper leaned against the counter. She wore no pants but had her shirt from the night before buttoned loosely around her. Genevieve opted for her usual threadbare sweats.

"What's next?" Genevieve said.

"Back to the bedroom?" Genevieve shot Harper a scolding look, and Harper revised her answer. "We take it one step at a time and keep things professional at work, save for a few stolen kisses here and there. I know I won't be able to resist."

"Me either. But you're the boss," Genevieve said with a wink. "I'll follow your lead." She thought about work. "And Clarissa?"

"I'll talk to her."

"Please don't. She already hates me." Genevieve dropped her head into her hands.

Harper knelt in front of Genevieve, pried her hands from her face, and forced her to look up. "Let me worry about Clarissa. I know her, I know how she thinks. If we continue like we're not together, it'll just add to the problem."

"I'm pretty sure she already knows something's going on between us."

"And I'll talk to her about it." Harper took Genevieve's hands in hers and smiled that damn soft smirk that Genevieve had fallen for months ago. "I have a meeting with a few investors on Monday morning about new content for this coming year. Clarissa is attending. I'll ask her to show up early so I can have a word with her. I promise you, the Clarissa problem will be solved as soon as possible."

Genevieve took a deep breath. "Fine." She stood and helped Harper to her feet. "Let's go back to bed so you can make me forget all about the outside world for the rest of the weekend." She led Harper by the hand to her bed.

"You're smart, beautiful, and want the same things in life that I do," Harper said. "How did I get so lucky?"

"You hired me." Genevieve smiled wickedly and pushed Harper onto her back across the mattress. They barely left the bedroom after that, and Genevieve forgot about the outside world waiting to devour them.

STEP TWENTY-TWO

Accept That Things Don't Always Work Out

Genevieve had no idea what to expect when Monday morning rolled around. She had reluctantly said good-bye to Harper late Sunday evening. After two consecutive sleepovers, waking up without the soft feel of Harper's skin touching hers was a lackluster start to Genevieve's day. Monday mornings were bad enough, but Genevieve was cranky because she didn't sleep well, nor did she get out of bed in time for her first cup of coffee. Two days with Harper affected her entire routine.

As Genevieve walked from her car to the office building, she tried to focus on the day ahead, the piece she had to write, and the conversation that should've taken place between Harper and Clarissa.

"Genevieve!" Harper called out.

"Harper?" Genevieve looked at her in confusion. The meeting was scheduled to start in five minutes, and she should have talked to Clarissa by now.

"I'm running so late this morning," Harper said, breathless from jogging to meet Genevieve. Harper kissed her before she reached for the door handle. "Good morning."

"Good morning," she said as they walked in together.

"Lunch today," Harper said as they came to a fork in the road—Genevieve's desk to the right and her office to the left. "I'll swing by your desk later." With a lopsided grin, Harper was gone.

When Genevieve arrived at her desk, she placed her jacket on the back of her office chair, unaware of the smile plastered across her face until Matthew caught a glimpse.

"My, my! Someone must've had a good weekend."

Genevieve heard him speak, but instead of acknowledging him, she chose to start up her computer and unpack her glasses and notebook from her bag. That didn't last long.

"Earth to Gen. Come in Gen!" He waved his hand in front of her eyes.

Genevieve pulled back, disgruntled, and swatted at his hand. "What?"

"What do you mean, 'what'? You walk in here looking like the pussy that ate the canary and expect me not to notice? Spill!"

"There's nothing to spill. I enjoyed my weekend off, and I'm excited to get to work." She shrugged nonchalantly, but her nervous bouncing leg gave her away.

Maxine sat beside her. "Good morning. I saw you walk in with Harper. Seems like everyone's running a little late today." Genevieve's eyes widened at Maxine's seemingly innocent words. When she turned back to Matthew, he was grinning devilishly.

"We arrived at the same time," Genevieve said. "We didn't come to work together."

"Oh my God, you're blushing."

Genevieve's face was on fire. She forgot exactly how she and Harper had planned to handle any discussion about their relationship at work, so she said the first thing that came to mind. "We're keeping it professional at work."

Maxine chuckled. "But not so much right outside of work." She winked.

Genevieve's head dropped. "You saw?"

"You two kiss without the help of mistletoe? Yes, I saw."

Genevieve covered her face and moaned.

"Listen, Gen, I'm happy for you, and I'm sure Matthew is too." Genevieve looked over to Matthew, who was in his own little world of self-satisfied amazement. "I've been waiting years to see Harper meet someone special. I'm glad it's you." Maxine clapped her hand on Genevieve's shoulder with an alarming amount of force. "Just keep her out of your column."

"I think I can manage that."

"Here comes Dana. Look busy!" Matthew said.

"Good morning, everyone!" Dana said cheerily. "Gen, Harper would like to see you in the meeting room."

"Why?" *Harper has a meeting with investors. Why would she want me there? Unless she wants to make my column bigger?* Genevieve smiled at the prospect of what this development could mean for her career.

"Not sure, but the meeting is about to start."

As much as she wanted to stop for coffee along the way, Genevieve didn't even pause. She didn't want to keep the investors waiting. When she stepped through the door, Harper greeted her silently with a broad smile. Genevieve looked around the room at the seven strangers, five women and two men. Clarissa sat at the head of the table. Genevieve opted to move to the side where Harper sat.

"You wanted to see me?"

"Actually, *I* did." Clarissa said. "Please have a seat, Gen." Clarissa pointed to the seat beside her and Genevieve sat nervously. "Shall we get started?"

Harper spoke up next. "I guess I'll start with wishing you all a Happy New Year." The sentiment was echoed around the table. Genevieve responded to the well wishes halfheartedly, keeping her attention on Clarissa. Her stomach cramped anxiously.

"With a New Year comes new content," Harper continued. "Every year I think we exceed our original plans for the magazine, and I don't expect this year to be any different." Harper looked at each one of the attendees separately, and Genevieve watched on in awe as she commanded the room. "Each of you has a different relationship with *Out Shore,* just as we have a different relationship with each of your niche markets. We're here to talk ideas, to think outside the box really, and to add something to *Out Shore* that'll help this magazine stand out from the rest." Harper looked at Genevieve for a moment before she nodded at Clarissa. "The first portion of the presentation is from Clarissa."

Clarissa smiled broadly. "Good morning." When she stood straight, her feminine appearance added a softness to her that kept her sharp edges well hidden. "What's one type of book always on the best-sellers list?" Clarissa looked around and waited for anyone to pitch an answer.

Harper politely played along and suggested, "Romances?" The room filled with quiet laughter.

"Well, yes, but I was thinking self-help books. How-to guides and the like. A lot of lost people in the world are desperate to find an instruction manual for life, and I think *Out Shore* can give it to them." Clarissa walked over to a laptop she had connected to a larger monitor. Everyone wore an excited expression, and even Harper seemed incredibly interested in what her ex-wife had in mind.

"I have a self-help book for just about everything," one of the female investors joked while they waited.

Clarissa motioned to Genevieve, and suddenly eight smiling faces were pointed at her. "I called in Genevieve

Applegate for one simple reason—I think she'll be the perfect person to head this new content."

"Really?" Genevieve and Harper said simultaneously.

"Yes, really," Clarissa said. "Let me introduce you all to what I hope will be our newest, most successful section yet: *Fake It till You Make It: A User's Guide.*"

Genevieve's curiosity and the little bit of confusion she may have felt slipped away as she took in the bold-lettered title across two pictures of her. On one side was a picture of her and Harper at the holiday party, and on the other was an old photo of Jeremy and Genevieve sharing a warm embrace. Harper looked at her with an expectant frown.

"Genevieve came to us from Pennsylvania where she was a straight girl in a *very* long-term relationship with her high school boyfriend. But something magical must've happened when she crossed the border into Jersey, because suddenly she was a young lesbian looking to live a big gay life." Clarissa's laughter was mirthless. "Clearly, she's the perfect person to help people lie their way to the top."

Harper stood abruptly and left the room. Genevieve went to run after her, but Clarissa stood in her way.

"Let me go!" Genevieve begged.

"I warned you, Gen. I don't want to see her hurt."

"Like how you hurt her?" Genevieve tried to maneuver around Clarissa, but the doorway was too narrow. "You had your chance."

"And you had your fun. You tried on the lesbian life for a while. I think it's time you go back to being a loser—"

Genevieve slapped Clarissa hard. Clarissa held her cheek and stumbled back as Genevieve looked on with wide eyes, her palm on fire. She had never hit anyone before, and as much as she would have liked to revel in the satisfaction, she had to catch up to Harper.

"Harper!" Genevieve called out as she ran between cubicles in search of her. She checked Harper's empty office and ran for the exit. She stepped out into the frigid winter morning and looked both ways down the street. She caught a glimpse of Harper rounding the corner and continued her chase. "Harper, wait!" She caught up to her quickly, but her sprint had left her out of breath when it came time to speak.

"What?"

"I'm sorry."

"You're sorry for what exactly? Lying to me? Making a fool out of me? Or getting caught?"

Genevieve flinched at Harper's uncharacteristically harsh tone, but the emptiness she saw in Harper's eyes hurt her the most.

"I didn't lie to you—well, at first I did," Genevieve said, stumbling through her excuse inarticulately. She shook her head in frustration, trying to gather her scattered thoughts.

"At first when you wanted me to hire you, you mean?"

"Yes!" Genevieve shivered as the cold bit her through her sweater. "It snowballed from there, but I haven't lied about us or my feelings for you."

"And what about Jeremy?"

"I *told* you we dated."

"When did you two break up?"

Genevieve's heart hammered in her throat. "Christmas Eve."

"Are you kidding me?" Harper erupted into maniacal laughter and started to pace. "I'm an idiot!"

"No, you're not."

"Yes, I *am*. And I *definitely* look like one to everyone in my own company." Harper went silent for a moment as she looked at the sky. When she looked at Genevieve again, small tears shimmered across her lower eyelids.

Genevieve's heart slowly shattered, not just for herself, but for causing Harper pain once again.

"We're done, you're fired." Harper headed back to the office building.

Genevieve's chin quivered. "What about forgetting the past? Did you mean any of that?"

Harper looked back at her, a fraction of her usual warmth hidden deep within a sad smile. "I meant it when I thought I knew you." She turned away, and tears trailed down Genevieve's cheeks.

Harper disappeared around the corner and Genevieve fell onto a nearby bench. She cried quietly to herself, no longer affected by the cold or the two strangers who watched from the other side of the street. She was numb to the temperature. She was numb to everything but the pain that echoed in her chest as her broken heart continued to beat.

Step Twenty-three

Reevaluate Your Plan

A large oak tree grew dangerously close to the window of Genevieve's childhood bedroom. It had served as the perfect escape when she was a rebellious teen who just wanted to spend a few more hours with Chloe or Jeremy, and it added to the ambience of spooky Halloween night sleepovers.

But Genevieve had forgotten how it would tap, tap, tap, against her window. The tree didn't care if it kept Genevieve awake when all she needed or wanted to do was sleep. Even on this sunny afternoon, Genevieve wanted nothing more than to close her eyes and forget, if only for a few hours, the horrid decisions she had made and the unthinkable pain she had caused.

Even when Tuesday morning rolled around, Genevieve declined her favorite breakfast foods and didn't want to call Chloe. She wanted none of it. She wanted this constant sadness and pain. She deserved it.

By Tuesday evening, almost a full thirty-six hours had passed since the last time Genevieve had anything more than small sips of water. Her head spun, and she felt weak when she sat up. She pulled herself from her twin bed, put on a pair of worn slippers, and walked downstairs. Her mother was in the kitchen, cleaning up remnants of the small, two-person meal she had fixed. She'd left a covered plate on the stove for Genevieve.

"Do we have juice?" Genevieve said. Her voice was gravelly and her throat was sore from crying.

Sandra twisted the dish towel around her hands. "No, honey. I'm sorry."

"I'll run and get some." Genevieve picked up her keys and went to the door slowly.

"Are you sure? I just mean, your hair is a bit of a mess."

"I'm just running to the corner store," Genevieve snapped impatiently. She needed to leave, needed to get out from under her mother's critical gaze. "Maybe when I get back I'll have dinner." Her mother smiled so brightly, Genevieve felt a fresh wave of sadness. "I'll be right back."

Genevieve stepped out into the fresh air, crying again the moment she was no longer surrounded by familiar smells. She sat in her car and waited for the engine to warm, shaking with chills and cries. She stared at the house, its lines and details distorted by tears. She thought about her mother's life. Was she lonely or just alone? After her parents' divorce, her mother had shown very little interest in meeting someone again, stating that her focus should be on her children, not on strange men. Genevieve felt hollow after losing Harper, and they had only shared a weekend together. What did her mom truly feel after all those years?

After a deep breath, Genevieve finally pulled out of the driveway and started on her way to the local convenience store. She continued to cry as she drove, marveling at how her body continued to produce tears. Genevieve missed the turn for the store.

"Dammit." She turned the wheel as far as it could go and performed a full U-turn in the middle of her neighborhood's main street. She didn't think twice because no one was around in Milan, never mind in the middle of winter. When she righted the car and continued on her mission for juice, blue and red lights flashed from behind her. "Seriously?" Genevieve rolled her wet eyes and pulled over.

The officer climbed out of his department issue sedan and approached her car. Genevieve was prepared with her window down and license and registration in hand.

"Do you know why I pulled you over?" said the bundled cop.

"Illegal U-turn?"

"You got…wait." The police officer bent down and peered into the car. "Gen?"

To Genevieve's chagrin, the officer was one of Jeremy's closest friends. "Hey, Pete."

"I didn't know you were back in town."

"My return was unexpected."

"Does Jeremy know you're visiting? How long are you in town for?" He fired off his questions rapidly, leaving Genevieve to wonder if he had just aced a course in interrogation techniques. "How's Jersey treating you? You look great!"

"Thanks. Um, Jeremy doesn't know I'm back, and I'm not sure how long I plan on staying."

"I bet you can't wait to get back to Jersey," he said excitedly. "I heard you're a big shot now."

Genevieve felt tears begin to well up again. She tried to rush the conversation along. "Are you going to write me a ticket?"

"Of course not! Jeez, Gen, you taught my baby sister how to ride a bike. How could I give you a ticket?" Pete scratched at the back of his neck.

Genevieve didn't expect to encounter kindness during this ride, and it hit her hard. Before she could rein in it, she started to cry again. The first sob that tore from her throat was so powerful, the burly police officer jumped. Pete reached hesitantly into the car window to pat Genevieve on the back.

"Are you okay?"

Genevieve cried harder and let loose every heavy thought that weighed on her heart and mind. "I lied during my job interview," she sobbed. "And my boss found out and I got fired!"

"Everyone lies during interviews."

She pinned him with her watery stare. "I said I was a lesbian, which now, ironically enough, seems to be fairly truthful, but that didn't matter to Harper."

"Harper?"

"That's my boss and my girlfriend—well, ex-girlfriend. She didn't know I was with Jeremy when she hired me and she found out thanks to her bitch of an ex-wife!" Genevieve reached into the compartment of her center console and pulled out a fast food napkin to blow her nose. "I tried to tell her the truth, but she insisted on forgetting the past." She blew her nose forcefully. "I wasn't lying to her, not after I knew I loved her."

Pete stood stunned. He looked back to his running police car and then again to Genevieve. "And what're you up to now?"

"I haven't eaten in days and all I wanted was juice. We don't have any juice…" Genevieve broke down into steady cries again.

"You really shouldn't drive in your condition, but let's get you some juice."

The police escort to and from the convenience store was a bit much, but Genevieve was eternally grateful to Pete for watching over her as she essentially stumbled across town. The flashing lights must've caught her mother's attention when Genevieve arrived back home because she came running out to the front porch before Genevieve got out of her car.

"Are you okay?" Her mother held her close and looked for wounds.

"I'm fine, Mom. That was just Pete."

"Oh." Sandra stepped back in relief. "Well, come on, I'll reheat your dinner."

"I think I'm just going to go back to bed." Genevieve shivered and held a large jug of cranberry juice closer to her chest. Retelling her tragic story, if even just a brief recap, to Pete had exhausted what little energy Genevieve had in her reserves.

"You have to eat."

"I will. Just not tonight. Tomorrow, I promise." She kissed her mother's cheek and went back up the stairs and climbed into bed.

The cranberry juice quenched Genevieve's thirst and hunger for sugar, but she regretted not having the foresight to get vodka along the way as well.

❖

The next morning felt a little easier for Genevieve. She took a long shower and only cried a little. She brushed her teeth and only zoned out into her reflection momentarily before getting back on track. She even put on the clean set of pajamas her mother left on the foot of her bed. Genevieve considered getting fully dressed for the day, but that would imply a readiness for the real world she definitely wasn't feeling yet. Her stomach growled from the smell of bacon wafting up from the kitchen.

She ran for the stairs, visualizing a large breakfast waiting

for her. By the time she reached the final step, she heard chitchat coming from the kitchen. Her mother was talking to someone, and that someone had a deep voice that sounded exactly like…

"Jeremy?" Genevieve rounded the corner into the kitchen, and she stared between her mother and ex-boyfriend quizzically.

"Hey, Gen," he said, standing quickly. Genevieve looked him up and down, suspicious of his presence and intentions. He was clean-shaven and dressed in a wrinkle-free polo and khakis, clothes he often wore for work, but the school day was already well under way. "Pete called me last night."

"Oh." Genevieve looked at a stack of pancakes and bacon on the stovetop. She was starving, but would she still have an appetite if Jeremy continued to talk? "Do you mind if I eat?"

"Please!" Sandra rushed to the stovetop and grabbed the plate. She placed it in front of Genevieve just as she sat, adding syrup and leaving to prepare a cup of coffee.

"What exactly did Pete tell you?" Genevieve said. She cut at her pancakes aggressively, tearing them into pieces instead of slicing. She stuffed her mouth with more than she was capable of chewing with ease.

Jeremy stared at Genevieve's overstuffed mouth with wide eyes. "Um, nothing much, just that you were back and seemed upset."

Genevieve added a bite of bacon to her still-full mouth.

"I wanted to check on you."

"I'm fine."

Sandra snorted and went back to cleaning up.

Jeremy reached across the small tabletop and grabbed Genevieve's hand, but she pulled back immediately. "Talk to me, Gen."

"I don't have anything to say, especially not to you." Maybe

Jeremy only remembered the positives of their relationship, but Genevieve mostly thought about their final conversation.

Jeremy sighed. "You're back, and that's what matters most. I think we should talk about what to do next."

"First off, I'm not 'back.'" Genevieve made finger quotes in the air. "And secondly, what do you mean 'we'?" She hooked her fingers again.

"You left Milan, Gen. You got out of here, and I think we can all agree that the world wasn't as nice to you as you expected it to be." Sandra left the kitchen in a hurry once Jeremy started to speak inclusively. "But you lived it, and now you know that this is where you belong." Jeremy reached into his pocket and pulled out a small velvet box. He placed it on the table and looked at Genevieve with large, hopeful eyes. "You belong here with me."

Genevieve felt panicked. "Oh, no."

"Oh, boy," Sandra said quietly.

Genevieve looked over Jeremy's shoulder at her mother. She was standing still in the doorway, and Genevieve pleaded with her eyes for her mother, her protector, to save her from this moment.

"Genevieve," Jeremy said. He stumbled through her full name, and Genevieve thought about how poetically the three syllables sounded when Harper said them. A pang of guilt sank deeper into her heart.

"Jeremy…" Genevieve shook her head.

"Will you marry me? Finally?" He smiled broadly, and the look in his eyes said he never expected Genevieve's life to be anything but him and this small town.

Without even opening it, Genevieve pushed the ring box away. "No."

"No?" Jeremy's smile fell.

"No! And I don't know why you thought I'd say yes!" Genevieve ran her fingers through her now-knotted hair. "I broke up with you because I have feelings for someone else."

Jeremy laughed.

"What's so funny?"

"Nothing. It's just…You move away on a whim and fall for someone unexpectedly?" Jeremy said in a mocking tone. "It's classic Gen—acting without thinking. If you just think for a minute, you'll see this is the life for you."

Genevieve took a deep calming breath. She *could* be irrational and too spontaneous for her own good. Her recent heartache was a constant reminder of that, but she had walked away from a life that no longer fit in order to find what was meant to be all along. She controlled her temper and tone. "You should go."

"Not without an answer."

"I gave you my answer!" Genevieve shouted.

"I think you should give it a little more thought."

"Oh my God, please shut up. I'm not a child who needs to be coached in making better decisions. I know what I want and what I don't want. I don't want to marry you." Genevieve watched her words register on Jeremy's face. He stood abruptly, his chair screeching across the floor.

"Just add this to your long list of terrible decisions." He stormed toward the front door, nearly knocking Sandra over. When he opened it, Chloe stood on the other side, poised to knock. She stepped aside wordlessly. His truck's exhaust roared as he sped away from the house.

"Was he always that much of an asshole?" Sandra said. She walked over and closed the front door behind Chloe.

"Yup." Genevieve shook her head. "And he wonders why I lied to land a job in New Jersey and fell in love with my female boss."

Sandra froze with her hand on the doorknob. "Oh, my…" She shook her head. "Let me put on another pot of coffee. I have a feeling I'm in for a very long story."

Genevieve ate two plates of pancakes and washed it all down with a large cup of coffee as she told everything from the beginning. She wasn't surprised when her mother asked questions like whether she made her bed before having Harper over and if Harper was as attractive as Chloe and Genevieve led her to believe. Chloe took out her phone and showed Sandra a picture from the *Out Shore* holiday party. Genevieve smiled when her mother's jaw dropped.

"Is that what's lurking in New Jersey? If so, I think I'm ready to move!" Sandra put on her colorful reading glasses and pulled Chloe's phone closer. "I'd have left Jeremy, too."

"See, Gen? Even your mother is unfazed by you falling for a chick," Chloe said.

"I didn't leave Jeremy because of Harper alone." Genevieve glared at Chloe. "She's a large part of it, yes, but Jeremy and I didn't fit anymore. It sounds terrible, but I outgrew him."

Sandra added her motherly insight then. "Sweetheart, I think it's safe to say you outgrew him a long time ago."

"Your mother's right, Gen."

"I know." Genevieve sat back into her chair with a huff.

After a beat of silence, Chloe asked the question Genevieve had been silently pondering since her arrival on her mother's doorstep. "What are you going to do next?"

"Eat more pancakes?" Genevieve said with a plastic smile.

"I'm serious, Gen. What are you going to do? Stay in Jersey? Move back here?"

"I really don't know. I have to find a new job, but I'm afraid of listing *Out Shore* as previous employment and having a potential employer ask why I left. What if they contact Harper as a reference?"

"Don't worry about that," Sandra said. "If everything you've told me about this woman is true, I believe she'd keep her personal feelings separate from her professional ones. You did a wonderful job while you worked for her, and that would surely shine through."

"Sandra's right. Just start applying and see what happens."

"But stay in Jersey," Sandra said. "You're obviously happier there."

Genevieve sipped at the remnants of her coffee and considered her mother's words carefully. Yes, she was happier in New Jersey. Her life in Asbury had been flourishing and lively, but how much of that happiness and promise relied on Harper and her job at *Out Shore*? Genevieve would have to head back to her apartment in order to find out.

Step Twenty-four

Travel Different Avenues

Genevieve arrived back at her apartment late on Thursday evening. She had left Pennsylvania with a new sense of determination to not let a breakup hinder her progress as a professional. If her short time at *Out Shore* had taught Genevieve anything, it was that she was a talented journalist, and her talent would not waver.

Upon her first step over the threshold, Genevieve noticed all the reminders of her time with Harper: dishes in the sink, sheets a mess, and the sweatshirt Harper had borrowed during her short stay thrown across the back of the couch. Genevieve's emotions started to take over. She felt desperation fueling her need to reach for her phone. One message, a short question asking whether Harper would be willing to spare a moment to listen—the desire to reach out burned in her fingertips. But Genevieve denied that temptation. She had to focus on herself.

She cleaned her apartment thoroughly, working long into the night. She stripped her bedding, did several loads of laundry, vacuumed, and dusted every surface she could reach. The next day was much of the same, except she dug a little deeper. She boxed up her issues of *Out Shore* for storage and swept every file on her computer devoted to her old job into one folder hidden within another folder on her desktop. Genevieve was serious about success this time, and she wanted little to no distractions.

Once her life and apartment were spotless, Genevieve took a seat in front of her computer, beer in hand, and started the next great job hunt. She read each listing *very* carefully and even logged onto each publication's website. This time around, Genevieve would research before applying. Before the night was over, she had sent out applications and resumes to several promising publications. She'd be happy with any job that would pay her bills at this point, but she hoped for one that would bring the sense of fulfillment she had only tasted while at *Out Shore*. She fell asleep missing Harper, much like she had each night before, but now she had a sense of optimism.

Three busy weeks passed. Genevieve had gone from one interview to the next, giving the same speech over and over, essentially selling herself as an experienced writer with a thirst for new experiences, but this tactic didn't seem to satisfy any of her potential employers. One older man told her that the stars in her "pretty blue eyes" told him she wouldn't make it in the obituaries business, while the woman who ran a small weekly nightlife magazine told Genevieve her style was too traditional and too personal, whatever that meant.

Good news didn't arrive until the end of February. An unknown number flashed on her phone screen.

"Hi, is this Genevieve Applegate?"

"Speaking."

"This is Joe Reynolds with *The Press*. We met earlier this week." Genevieve contained her giddy excitement. She remembered the caller and the interview quite well. He was kind, she had nailed every question with a perfect answer, and the job sounded like something out of a dream. "Regarding the job for our travel and leisure section?" His tone conveyed worry, and Genevieve realized she hadn't said a word.

"Yes, Mr. Reynolds." Genevieve was unsure what else to say. *It's nice to hear from you? Please hire me, I'm desperate? I remember the interview well because I almost threw up from nerves?* She opted for a general pleasantry. "How are you?"

"I'm doing very well, and I think you will be, too, in a moment." Genevieve could hear the smile in his voice, and her heart beat faster with excitement. "Genevieve, I'm calling to let you know we've narrowed down our search to you and one other applicant, but I'm feeling pretty positive you'll be our newest staff member."

As much as she wanted to bask in the happiness of the moment, Genevieve hesitated. "If you don't mind me asking, Mr. Reynolds, why are you calling me before your final decision?"

He laughed heartily. "That's a fair question. I normally wouldn't, but like I said, I feel pretty confident that you're our choice. We just have to follow up on references, and we'll call you back in for a final interview. The reason I'm calling you now is because once you're hired, you'll be sent to Montreal, Canada, on your first assignment almost immediately. Do you have a passport, Genevieve?"

Her head started spinning. "No…"

"If you start the process now, you should get it just in time. I'll be in touch soon."

"Thank you." No sooner were the words out of her mouth than the call was ended.

Genevieve finally started to believe her success had less to do with Harper or her former job and more with her talent as a writer. She was on the brink of landing a job most journalists would be willing to lie or kill for. *The Press* had been wanting to revamp their paper, which included not only more columns, but a real travel and leisure section, complete with journalists actually traveling and enjoying the leisure, mostly on the company's dime.

What did all of this mean to Genevieve? Her home life would be based in New Jersey, but she'd be flying around the world, away from the shambles of her personal life, and getting to write about it. Mr. Reynolds said in their interview that the position and department were experimental at this time. They wanted to make sure it would be cost effective and successful before naming it a permanent section, but Genevieve was happy to take the risk, even if only for a few short months.

Genevieve sat at her computer and opened her favorite search engines. When she started typing, the recent search bar dropped and she saw the words "lesbian sex." She smiled sadly before deleting her search history and typing *how to get a passport.*

The next week flew by, and March felt much colder than February did. On Sunday evening, Genevieve was preparing for her final interview with *The Press*. She was equal parts confident and nervous. Her passport was ready, and she had purchased new luggage two days before. She checked off her list of things she needed to get before taking on her new job, and she jotted down positive thoughts in the margin.

A knock at her door startled her. She gasped when she looked through the small peephole. Although her unexpected guest stood with her head down, Genevieve would have recognized Harper anywhere. She opened the door and stared at Harper blankly.

After a moment's silent standoff, Harper finally offered a small greeting. "Hi."

"Hi." Genevieve crossed her arms over her chest and leaned against the door frame. She tried to act casual, distant even, but so much more was happening in her head and her heart. Genevieve might have been ready to start a new job and travel out of the country, but she wasn't ready to see Harper again.

"I'm sorry to just stop by like this. I'm sure you're probably busy."

"I am, actually."

"I wanted to talk to you." Harper cleared her throat and looked past Genevieve into her apartment. "Can we go inside?"

Genevieve didn't want to. She didn't want to let this woman into her life just to watch her walk out of it again, but she didn't want her neighbors in her business either. "Fine," Genevieve said, stepping aside. Harper went right for the couch after taking off her bulky jacket.

"It's been so cold lately," Harper said awkwardly.

"It has been." Genevieve sat in her computer chair and faced Harper. She needed to maintain her distance if she wanted to keep her wits about her. Seeing Harper revived a storm of emotions within her. Even though she still felt an overwhelming sense of pain over their split, she also found an unexpected rush of happiness. Genevieve shook away those thoughts. "What did you want to talk about?"

"I received two very interesting phone calls this week. The first was from *The Press*, asking about your work with *Out Shore* and how I'd rate you as a staff member."

Genevieve fidgeted nervously.

"Don't worry. I gave you a glowing recommendation. You were the best writer I've hired since Maxine." They shared a small laugh before Harper grew serious again. "The second call was a bit more of a surprise."

Genevieve racked her brain for who it could've been, but she was coming up short. "Who?"

"Your mother."

"My mother?"

"Yes, your mother. Sandra is a very charming woman."

Genevieve thought of her mother standing in her decorative rooster-cluttered kitchen in a worn apron and tried to picture that as charming. "What did my mother have to say?"

"That I'm an idiot. Well, to be exact, she told me that I'm a gorgeous idiot."

Genevieve covered her reddening face with her hands.

"She told me how smart and caring and how wonderful you are, and she told me that I have no idea what I'm missing out on by walking away from you."

"Harper, I am so sorry. I can't make enough excuses for my mother, but really I don't think she knows any better than to be overly invasive."

"It's okay, really. We had a good conversation about trust and relationships. She told me about her divorce and I told her about mine. It was very therapeutic."

Genevieve raised her eyebrow skeptically.

"I told her that I do know exactly what I'm missing, but I don't know how to trust you again."

Genevieve swallowed against the tightness in her throat. "And what did my mom say to that?"

"She told me that if trusting you again was something I wanted, then I'd have to talk to you about it."

"Where was this wise advice when I was a teenager?" Genevieve said, trying to distract her from an errant tear that fell down her cheek.

"She must've been storing it away for the big moments," Harper said with a laugh before looking Genevieve in the eye. "How do I trust you again? Can I trust you again?"

Genevieve reigned in her eagerness. She took a long breath before answering. "You can. I may have lied about my circumstances, but I didn't lie about who I was." Genevieve took another deep breath. "And I never lied about my feelings for you." They shared a silent look for a moment too long, and the atmosphere grew uncomfortable. Harper stood and put on her jacket.

"I should go." Harper walked to the door with Genevieve hot on her heels. She turned back and said, "I want to trust you again, but I need time." They were standing within a foot of each other, and Genevieve felt the same pull she always had toward Harper. She looked up into her clear gray eyes and felt a weakness that twisted her insides pleasantly.

"Of course," Genevieve agreed readily, even though she had no idea what Harper meant by *needing time*.

"And I want you back at *Out Shore*. I know you have an incredible opportunity lined up, and I wouldn't blame you for hopping on a plane to get away from the drama, but your fans miss you."

"My fans?" Half of her focus was on Harper's words while the other half was divided between her request to come back to the magazine and looking at Harper's full lips.

"Your readers have been emailing nonstop asking when the next update to your column was coming. I haven't responded to any yet."

"My readers miss me?" Genevieve said in wonderment. She never really expected to have a devoted following.

"They do, and I think even Matthew misses having you around." Harper shot her a lopsided grin.

Genevieve bit her lower lip and looked away. Her heart was telling her to go back, to be present every day and use that as a way to win Harper's trust again, but her head was singing a different tune. Would she be able to respect Harper's need for time while working side by side five days a week?

She whispered out the two hardest words she'd ever spoken. "I can't."

Harper nodded solemnly. "Of course."

"It's not that I don't want to, but—"

"I get it, Genevieve. Who would turn down a job that'll take you all over the world for one where you stare at the same ocean every day?" Harper leaned in and kissed her cheek. She let her lips linger slightly, just long enough to whisper her parting words close to Genevieve's ear. "Good night, Genevieve." Harper turned away from Genevieve and was out the door in a rush.

Genevieve stood in her open doorway well after Harper had departed. She replayed their conversation over and over in her head, but that only served to intensify the pain. Harper thought *Out Shore* was second-choice material, when in reality it'd be Genevieve's first choice every time.

She was just trying to use her head for once.

STEP TWENTY-FIVE

If You Fail, Start from the Beginning

Genevieve bounced her knee up and down nervously. Time hadn't moved much since she last checked, but the last thirteen seconds felt like an hour to Genevieve. She had never expected to be starting a new job again within six months, and it was just as nerve wrecking the second time. No, her first day at *Out Shore* was a cakewalk compared to this.

The Press occupied two floors of an aged office building in the heart of Asbury. The artificial lighting and bland decorations reminded Genevieve of her former offices at the *Sunrise*.

Distance and time, Genevieve reminded herself. The most important outcome of this whole mess was a potential reconciliation with Harper. Harper would have the time she needed, and this job would give Genevieve the distance necessary to grant Harper her request. If she had returned to *Out Shore* like Harper had wanted, Genevieve would have been incapable of keeping a clear mind. She'd probably dive headfirst into yet another irrational action.

Not again, Genevieve scolded herself and looked at the clock again. This time she was mildly satisfied that two minutes had passed. Joe Reynolds should be calling her in at any moment, and he would give her details about her first destination piece.

A few women walked by where Genevieve sat in the hallway, but she didn't receive even the slightest side-eye. Even the difference in attitude was obvious. The space was quiet, women were dressed in monochromatic workday attire, and the men wore tired trousers with shirts and ties. Genevieve smoothed her moist palms along her thighs.

"Genevieve?" Mr. Reynolds said from his office doorway. Genevieve hadn't even heard him open the door. She looked up at him with wide eyes and a fake smile. "Come in."

Joe Reynolds's office was as dark, cold, and impersonal as Harper's was warm and friendly.

"I hope you didn't have any troubles finding the office."

"I found it without a problem," Genevieve lied. She had arrived on the wrong floor twice before finally finding where the executive offices were, and she had to ask three less-than-friendly people where to find Mr. Reynolds. "It's an impressive building."

"It could use some updates, but it works for now." They stared blankly at each other after sharing a small smile. He nodded slightly, and Genevieve wondered if he had forgotten he was leading this meeting. "So, I have some new hire paperwork for you to fill out." Joe placed a blue folder on the desktop. "Tax forms, personal information, all the good stuff." He handed a series of papers to Genevieve.

"I thought this was a final interview."

He smiled broadly. "I wasn't kidding when I said you'd likely be our choice," he said. "I got the go-ahead this morning from my boss to hire you."

"Wow." Genevieve released a long breath. She looked over the forms.

Each page asked her basic information, a few asked for her Social Security number, and the final page was a contract of employment.

"I know it seems daunting, but once these are all filled out, we can move on to the fun stuff—Montreal." He motioned through the air with his hands as if the word would appear on a floating banner.

"Right, Montreal." Genevieve breathed deeply. She grabbed a pen from the cup on Mr. Reynolds's desk and started to scribble her answers into the blanks. Every sheet was easy until she reached the contract. Her work, all of her intellectual property really, would be the property of *The Press*. She looked at him.

"Just a formality," he assured her. "A few years ago we had a columnist who reported back to one of our competitors with our every move."

"Sounds like some serious espionage for local newspapers."

He shrugged. "Competition is competition. Anyway, you leave tomorrow. Here's a list of stops we'd like you to visit and highlight in your write-up."

Genevieve looked at the pamphlet he handed her. She hadn't noticed how much she was shaking until the sounds of pages smacking together filled the cramped office. Was this really what she wanted? It was the sound decision, yes, but since when did Genevieve Applegate ever make sound decisions?

"I cannot apologize enough, Mr. Reynolds, but I don't think this position is right for me," Genevieve said quietly. "I'm sorry." She stood and pushed her purse onto her shoulder.

"You haven't even worked a day yet."

"I don't have to." She smiled at him kindly. "There's

another position I think would fit me better." She was out the door before he could say more.

Genevieve drove directly to her apartment to change.

❖

Genevieve strode through the large, clear doors of *Out Shore* and paused long enough to allow the moment to wash over her. Spontaneous or well planned out, what the hell difference did it make when it came to the perfect job and love?

A small smile lit up Genevieve's face as she approached Dana's desk. Expectedly, Dana was working diligently on some paperwork before her. Genevieve cleared her throat and straightened the collar of her green blouse. "Is Ms. Davies available?"

Dana looked up at Genevieve, and for only the second time in their working relationship, her professional exterior slipped. "She's, uh, in her office. Y-you can go right in, Gen."

Genevieve smiled at her uncharacteristic stutter. "Thank you."

When she walked into Harper's office that Monday morning, a pleasant sense of déjà vu washed over her, and she hoped Harper would feel the same. Harper was chatting with someone on the phone, her back was to the door, and Genevieve knew she was likely staring at the calm ocean as she spoke. Genevieve stood before Harper's desk and waited.

"Thank you very much, Chris." Harper spun her chair around and jumped noticeably at Genevieve's sudden presence. She kept her eyes on Genevieve as she ended her call. "I look forward to participating at this year's event. We'll talk soon. Take care." She hung up and smiled up at Genevieve. "Hey."

Genevieve reached out her hand. "Good morning, Ms. Davies. I'm here to interview for the available position."

"You don't have to do that."

"My name is Genevieve Applegate." Genevieve kept her hand outstretched until Harper took it. "It's a pleasure to meet you, Ms. Davies."

"Have a seat. And please call me Harper."

Genevieve released a slow breath when Harper started to play along. She was willing to embarrass herself on a regular basis, but she didn't want to make Harper uncomfortable.

"Harper, I've heard a lot about you and *Out Shore,* and I have to say that it's a dream come true to even be considered for the position." Genevieve turned on her charm and removed her black blazer.

Harper looked at her emerald green blouse, and a smile of recognition lit up her face. "That's a lovely blouse," she said. "Would you mind me asking what the material is?"

"It's a silk blend."

"I'd be afraid of it staining from perspiration, you know, in high-pressure situations," Harper said with a smirk.

"It's my lucky interview blouse. The last time I wore it I landed a job that changed my whole life."

"What happened?"

"I made a few uncharacteristic mistakes that led to my termination. I'm sure that's not what you want to hear as a potential employer, but I'm not the type to lie in order to get what I want in life."

Harper nodded as the silence stretched on, filling the room with familiar tension and unspoken feelings. "Genevieve, I don't have to tell you how important *Out Shore* is to me and that I take its success very seriously. I want this magazine to be *very* successful." Harper leveled a steely gaze at Genevieve, taking the same position she had in their first interview. "What can you bring to the table that'll help make that happen?"

"An honest perspective," Genevieve said simply.

"Why do you want to work here?" Harper said in a less confident voice, and she stared at her folded hands on the desktop, seemingly comparing her thumbs. Genevieve knew this was it: Harper was asking every unspoken question in seven simple words.

"Because I believe in this magazine, and I believe I can use my life experiences to not only help readers learn about themselves, but also come to accept the person they've been all along."

"How so?"

"I was in a relationship with a man for many years—too many years—and I stayed because I didn't believe in anything more than average. I'm from a very small town where most people married their high school sweethearts and followed in their parents' footsteps when it came to work. That's the average life expected of everyone." Genevieve shifted to sit on the edge of her seat.

"What changed for you?"

"I was ready for a more exciting life."

Harper deflated.

Genevieve smiled and added, "And I fell in love with an amazing woman."

Harper's head shot up, her pewter eyes wide.

"My feelings for her exceed average and certainly weren't expected," she said, and she giggled before continuing. "And she definitely added excitement to my life." Genevieve stood and walked around Harper's desk, looking down at the woman who had brought her to life so many months ago.

"I'm Genevieve Applegate, a woman from Milan,

Pennsylvania, who chased the fulfillment of professional success to New Jersey. I told a few lies along the way, to myself and others, and I'm sorry for the pain they have caused." Genevieve swallowed roughly and looked out the windows to the rolling ocean for strength to continue. When she looked into Harper's eyes again, she saw the same powerful calm there. She could think of worse things than looking at either every day for the rest of her life.

"I'm so sorry for hurting you, but I can't say I regret doing what I did." Genevieve flashed a watery smile and laughed through a cry. Harper stood and wiped stray tears from Genevieve's cheeks. Her face was set in a soft smile, and Genevieve took her first easy breath since that fateful Monday morning.

Harper looked at Genevieve. She tilted her head and said, "Why not?" She stepped closer to Genevieve, pinning her against the edge of her desk.

"Because it brought me to you." Genevieve took hold of Harper's lower back, balling Harper's shirt in her fists. "I know you said you needed time, but you also said you hated salads. I didn't listen then, and I don't think I should listen now."

Harper laughed and shook her head. She leaned forward and brought her lips within millimeters of Genevieve's. "Always disregarding my words." Harper's joke fell flat when Genevieve pulled back and looked at her seriously.

"No more lies," Genevieve pleaded. "I promise."

"I know." Harper moved back a step. That small distance felt like an infinite chasm to Genevieve and she whined dramatically. Harper laughed even louder. "You're hired. You got the job and the girl, there's no reason to lie."

"I got the girl?" Genevieve said in awe.

"She's all yours."

"You needed time."

"I don't need time." Harper framed Genevieve's face in her hands. "I just need you." Harper kissed her sweetly.

Genevieve's knees buckled, and she fell fully against the desk, the furniture holding her up as she reacquainted herself with Harper's wondrous mouth.

Once they separated, Genevieve took a bit longer to grasp her bearings and speak again. She watched the colors shift from grays to blues in Harper's eyes, and she lost herself in the emotion of the moment. A commotion outside the office door brought her back to reality.

"What about Clarissa?" Genevieve said.

"You don't have to worry about Clarissa."

"You fired her?"

Harper shook her head. "I got a little inspiration when I heard about the job you were being offered, and I decided to start a new department and column here. Clarissa is the new head of Travel and Leisure." Genevieve's smile grew larger as the idea set in. "She'll be on the road most of the time, reporting on gay-friendly hot spots across the country."

"How did she take that news?"

"Very well, after we had a screaming match about the stunt she pulled during the investors' meeting," Harper said. "I think she needed a break just as much as I did. To be honest, I'm hoping this change benefits her. Maybe while she's meeting new people, she can find herself along the way."

"Maybe she'll find her Miss Right."

"If it happened for me, then anything's possible."

Genevieve wrapped her arms around Harper and held her in a nearly painful embrace. Her future seemed limitless now. "I have to get to work." She stepped away and walked to the door.

Harper called her back. "Wait!"

Genevieve turned back to see Harper stand with her palms turned up.

"I didn't even get a chance to tell you that I love you, too."

Genevieve's heart swelled. She ran back for a quick kiss and said, "Tell me later over dinner." She grinned and left the office, nearly running into Dana, who stood just outside the door.

"I'm happy you're back, Gen," Dana said sheepishly, barely making eye contact.

"I am too, Dana." Genevieve walked off with her head high, determined to be the very best—for herself and for Harper.

When Genevieve sat at her old desk twenty minutes later, Matthew caught her up on all the office drama she had missed while she was gone, most of which revolved around Clarissa and her new position. She looked to her left and saw Maxine smiling at her. Not one of them asked about her lies. They displayed no malice as they welcomed her back, and they both seemed genuinely happy she occupied the spot between them once again. Genevieve popped a gummy bear from one of the nine bags left in her desk drawer into her mouth when she watched Harper walk past their desks. They shared a coy, knowing smile. Harper nearly stumbled when Genevieve added a wink.

It had all started with a spontaneous lie, followed by many trials and tribulations, but step by step, Genevieve was able to create a reality she was proud of. She could finally say that she had made it.

ALWAYS CELEBRATE YOUR SUCCESS

Eighteen months later

Genevieve didn't expect to be having an engagement party just six months after moving in with Harper. But then again, when they lay sprawled across the sofa on a rainy July afternoon, Genevieve didn't expect Harper to propose either.

Harper's proposal had easily become her favorite memory to lose herself in. Harper said the desire to get married didn't come from a traumatic catalyst this time. Harper told her she wanted every boring day and every other moment of their lives to feel as special as that one. Marrying Genevieve was the only way Harper could have that. Genevieve cried for an hour straight, all while laughing and saying "yes" more times than she could count.

She took a break from deciding between the seven dresses she had laid out across the bed to admire her two-carat diamond solitaire, entranced by its sparkling and abundant facets.

"Are you staring at your ring again?" Harper said from behind her.

"I can't help it, it's so beautiful." Genevieve stepped into Harper's arms. She wore only her bra and panties, but Harper was fully dressed.

"Now you know why you always catch me staring at you."

"I already said yes. You don't have to keep sweet-talking me," Genevieve said, wrapping her arms around Harper's neck.

"I still have to get you to the altar. Why aren't you dressed yet?"

Genevieve smiled shyly. "I can't decide which one to wear. Imagine what I'll be like when I'm shopping for my wedding dress."

"We'll never be getting married," Harper deadpanned, earning a pinch from Genevieve.

Genevieve shuffled through her choices again, holding each up beside Harper for comparison. Tonight was about them, so their appearance mattered more than usual. Feeling Harper grip her backside was a great distraction.

"I need to get dressed, and you aren't helping." Genevieve pushed back against Harper's hands, hoping one would caress between her legs. When the touch she craved didn't come, Genevieve stood and leaned back against Harper.

"I'm much better at helping you take your clothes off, not putting them on," Harper whispered into her ear as she ran her palms over Genevieve's abdomen.

No matter how much time had passed, Harper's words and touch still demolished Genevieve's resolve. She spun in Harper's arms.

"You have ten minutes, otherwise we'll be late to our own party."

"I'm taking fifteen." Harper lifted Genevieve and sat her on a nearby dresser. She kissed Genevieve's throat and then the valley between her breasts. "Dana's always early, and she'll entertain everyone until we get there."

"Wait," Genevieve said, pushing Harper away gently. "I thought they weren't coming back until tonight."

"Dana sent me a message earlier, saying that she didn't want to miss the party."

"Does that mean Clarissa is coming, too?" Genevieve rushed to pick a dress and put it on, no longer caring which one.

"I received a message from her as well. She's bringing someone special."

"How'd that come up?"

"It didn't. I got one message from Dana, and then one from Clarissa right afterward, and that's all it said. I think it's nice that she wanted us to know."

Genevieve was shocked. "Do you think it's someone she met in Cabo?" she said, referencing Clarissa's latest *Out Shore* trip.

Harper shrugged. "I have no idea. I doubt it, though. She was supposed to spend her time sightseeing, not just having raucous sex with locals. That's the whole reason I sent Dana with her—to keep her on a tight leash."

"Even Dana isn't *that* much of a miracle worker." Genevieve touched up her light makeup in the vanity mirror before turning back to Harper. "How do I look? Worthy of your eternal love?"

"You look worthy of my eternal awe." Harper kissed Genevieve's cheek before raising her left hand to her lips. "You're breathtaking."

"And you look dashing as usual." Genevieve smoothed her hands down the front of Harper's sky blue, short-sleeved button-up. The color complemented her magenta dress.

"Ready?"

"Just need shoes." Genevieve rushed to their closet and returned with two sets of heels. "Strappy sandals or classic pumps?" she said, holding them up in front of Harper's face.

"You always complain when you wear the sandals."

"But they're perfect for summer," Genevieve whined. "I'm wearing the sandals."

Harper smiled and watched her strap on her shoes. Genevieve knew she wanted to make a comment, but she held out her hand for Genevieve to take instead and asked if she was ready to go.

Genevieve gripped Harper's hand tightly. "Ready as I'll ever be."

❖

The Blue Bar was the perfect place to have their engagement party. Festivities were in full swing by the time Genevieve and Harper arrived. The setting was decorated with modern touches, the staff was tattooed and pleasant, and the eclectic space overlooked the ocean. Genevieve had fallen in love the first time she stepped foot in the bar, and every time after was just as wonderful.

"Would you like me to get you a beer?" Harper said, grazing the shell of Genevieve's ear with her lips.

"No. In celebration, I'd like to try something different tonight. I'm going to order a mojito."

"I'll order a beer. Just in case."

Genevieve waited for Harper to get their drinks before meeting their group out on the reserved patio space. Harper got the young female bartender's attention easily. Genevieve noticed the bartender looking her over, and she bristled when the bartender reached out to touch Harper's forearm.

"Calm down, killer. I can see the steam coming out of your ears from here."

Genevieve spun around. "Chloe!" Genevieve hugged her briefly before looking back at the bar. "She's touching her, and I don't like it."

"She's also working for tips, and Harper is very easy to flirt with. Need I mention your mother's display of affection at Christmastime?"

"No, and please don't ever again. Now look at my ring and squeal like a true best friend and maid of honor."

Chloe obeyed with a dramatic display of excitement that got the attention of every other patron in their area.

"I guess my intuition to order a drink for Chloe was accurate," Harper said as she returned to Genevieve with an extra mojito in hand. "Genevieve wanted to try something new, and I ordered you the same because I know you'll drink anything."

"She's thoughtful *and* remembers all the most important things about me. She really is a keeper, Gen."

"I know." Genevieve wanted to say more, but she saw a very tan Dana approaching. "Dana! Nice tan." She hugged Dana briefly. "I'm happy you made it back in time."

"Thank you, and there was no way I'd miss this." Dana said, her eyes only on Genevieve. "We're all out on the patio, waiting for the guests of honor to arrive."

"Is Clarissa here?" Genevieve said, her hand cupped around her mouth conspiratorially.

Dana nodded like a bobblehead doll before answering. "Yes, yes, she is. But you, Gen, should focus on yourself and not others. Tonight is about celebrating the love *you* found unexpectedly." She grabbed Harper's hand and then Genevieve's and gave them a less-than-gentle tug. "Come on."

Genevieve looked back at Chloe and then at Harper oddly as she dragged them along. When they arrived at the doorway that separated the patio from the indoors, every face from *Out Shore* greeted them with broad smiles. They shouted a robust round of congratulations and Matthew popped a cork from a champagne bottle, causing Genevieve to shriek.

"Get your bubbly, ladies." Matthew handed them each a champagne flute before holding his own up. "A toast to our amazing boss and the most beautiful flower the backwoods of Pennsylvania has ever produced. Your love makes me believe that maybe I'll fall in love one day, just not anytime soon because there's at least three guys—"

"Matthew!" Maxine scolded.

"To love!" He held up his glass and everyone followed.

"Thank you, Matthew." Harper touched her glass to his and then to Genevieve's before sipping her champagne.

Genevieve looked at the glass in her hand and back to Harper in a panic. Was it bad luck to *not* drink after toasting your own engagement? She looked around the crowd, and as everyone else finished off their champagne, she nonchalantly set her glass on the outdoor bar top. A flash of red hair from the end of the bar caught her attention.

Clarissa looked good, as expected, but she appeared to be in a heated discussion with someone hidden by a poorly placed support beam. Clarissa's face was void of any anger, many softer emotions playing within her expressions. Genevieve craned her neck to see who Clarissa was talking to. The other person *had* to be her "someone special." Clarissa looked down as she spoke, which led Genevieve to surmise her date was shorter. Once Clarissa took her date's hand and kissed it tenderly, Genevieve felt like a voyeur and forced her eyes away.

"Genevieve?" Harper said.

"What?"

"Chloe wants to know if you plan on drinking your mojito, because she wants it."

Genevieve took a healthy sip of her drink, fully prepared to hate it, but she was surprised at the minty lime concoction. "This is delicious."

"Damn." Chloe snapped her fingers and stalked off toward the bar.

Genevieve checked her surroundings before saying to Harper, "Look straight ahead."

"Okay. What am I looking at?"

"Clarissa."

"I see her."

"She's talking to her date. Can you see them?"

"I see Clarissa, but she's only talking to Dana."

"That's impossible. Just a few seconds ago, Clarissa was kissing someone's hand." Genevieve turned around, and the realization hit her immediately when she recognized the watch on Dana's wrist. "Holy shit. Clarissa and Dana."

"No way."

"Way," Matthew chimed in. "I didn't think it was possible either." He picked up Genevieve's untouched champagne and walked away.

"Wow." Genevieve couldn't stop watching Dana cozy up to Clarissa, and the way Clarissa noticeably softened.

"They make sense." Harper wrapped her arms around Genevieve's waist and nuzzled the crook of her neck.

"I'm dying to know how it happened."

"This *is* Clarissa we're talking about. I'm sure we'll all get to read about it in the next issue of *Out Shore*." She bit lightly at Genevieve's earlobe. "Until then, let's celebrate us." Harper started to sway them in time to the music that floated throughout the sea air.

Genevieve turned in Harper's arms and framed her face with her hands. "I plan on spending the rest of my life celebrating us." She leaned up and kissed Harper. Genevieve teetered on her high sandals and one of her ankles gave out. Harper caught her before she fell.

"Thanks for catching me."

"I always will, and I'll make sure to always have ice packs in the freezer."

Harper's smile was brilliant and Genevieve's laugh, unrestrained. They danced and celebrated along with friends, coworkers, and loved ones in the setting summer sun. Genevieve had never known contentment like this. She had never expected to love, or be loved, in such an overwhelming way. Life truly had a funny way of unfolding for a dreamer like Genevieve Applegate. And if Genevieve was certain of anything in that moment, it was that vowing to love Harper until her dying day would be the easiest step to take along the way.

About the Author

M. Ullrich has always called New Jersey home and currently resides by the beach with her wife and three boisterous felines. After many years of regarding her writing as just a hobby, the gentle yet persistent words of encouragement from her wife pushed M. Ullrich to take a leap into the world of publishing. Much to her delight and amazement, that world embraced her.

By day, M. Ullrich works full-time in the optical field and spends most of her days off working on her writing. When her pen isn't furiously trying to capture her imagination (a rare occasion), she enjoys being a complete entertainer. Whether she's telling an elaborate story or a joke or getting up in front of a crowd to sing and dance her way through her latest karaoke selection, M. Ullrich will do just about anything to make others smile. She also happens to be fluent in three languages: English, sarcasm, and TV/movie quotes.

Books Available From Bold Strokes Books

Complications by MJ Williamz. Two women battle for the heart of one. (978-1-62639-769-9)

Crossing the Wide Forever by Missouri Vaun. As Cody Walsh and Lillie Ellis face the perils of the untamed West, they discover that love's uncharted frontier isn't for the weak in spirit or the faint of heart. (978-1-62639-851-1)

Fake It till You Make It by M. Ullrich. Lies will lead to trouble, but can they lead to love? (978-1-62639-923-5)

Girls Next Door, edited by Sandy Lowe and Stacia Seaman. Best-selling romance authors tell it from the heart—sexy, romantic stories of falling for the girls next door. (978-1-62639-916-7)

Pursuit by Jackie D. The pursuit of the most dangerous terrorist in America will crack the lines of friendship and love, and not everyone will make it out from under the weight of duty and service. (978-1-62639-903-7)

The Practitioner by Ronica Black. Sometimes love comes calling whether you're ready for it or not. (978-1-62639-948-8)

Unlikely Match by Fiona Riley. When an ambitious PR exec and her super-rich coding geek-girl client fall in love, they learn that giving something up may be the only way to have everything. (978-1-62639-891-7)

Where Love Leads by Erin McKenzie. A high school counselor and the mom of her new student bond in support of the troubled girl, never expecting deeper feelings to emerge, testing the boundaries of their relationship. (978-1-62639-991-4)

Forsaken Trust by Meredith Doench. When four women are murdered, Agent Luce Hansen must regain trust in her most valuable investigative tool—herself—to catch the killer. (978-1-62639-737-8)

Letter of the Law by Carsen Taite. Will federal prosecutor Bianca Cruz take a chance at love with horse breeder Jade Vargas, whose dark family ties threaten everything Bianca has worked to protect—including her child? (978-1-62639-750-7)

New Life by Jan Gayle. Trigena and Karrie are having a baby, but the stress of becoming a mother and the impact on their relationship might be too much for Trigena. (978-1-62639-878-8)

Royal Rebel by Jenny Frame. Charity director Lennox King sees through the party-girl image Princess Roza has cultivated, but will Lennox's past indiscretions and Roza's responsibilities make their love impossible? (978-1-62639-893-1)

Unbroken by Donna K. Ford. When Kayla and Jackie, two women with every reason to reject Happily Ever After, fall in love, will they have the courage to overcome their pasts and rewrite their stories? (978-1-62639-921-1)

Where the Light Glows by Dena Blake. Mel Thomas doesn't realize just how unhappy she is in her marriage until she meets Izzy Calabrese. Will she have the courage to overcome her insecurities and follow her heart? (978-1-62639-958-7)

Her Best Friend's Sister by Meghan O'Brien. For fifteen years, Claire Barker has nursed a massive crush on her best friend's older sister. What happens when all her wildest fantasies come true? (978-1-62639-861-0)

Escape in Time by Robyn Nyx. Working in the past is hell on your future. (978-1-62639-855-9)

Forget-Me-Not by Kris Bryant. Is love worth walking away from the only life you've ever dreamed of? (978-1-62639-865-8)

Highland Fling by Anna Larner. On vacation in the Scottish Highlands, Eve Eddison falls for the enigmatic forestry officer Moira Burns despite Eve's best friend's campaign to convince her that Moira will break her heart. (978-1-62639-853-5)

Phoenix Rising by Rebecca Harwell. As Storm's Quarry faces invasion from a powerful neighbor, a mysterious newcomer with powers equal to Nadya's challenges everything she believes about herself and her future. (978-1-62639-913-6)

Soul Survivor by I. Beacham. Sam and Joey have given up on hope, but when fate brings them together it gives them a chance to change each other's life and make dreams come true. (978-1-62639-882-5)

Strawberry Summer by Melissa Brayden. When Margaret Beringer's first love Courtney Carrington returns to their small town, she must grapple with their troubled past and fight the temptation for a very delicious future. (978-1-62639-867-2)

The Girl on the Edge of Summer by J.M. Redmann. Micky Knight accepts two cases, but neither is the easy investigation it appears. The past is never past—and young girls lead complicated, even dangerous lives. (978-1-62639-687-6)

Unknown Horizons by CJ Birch. The moment Lieutenant Alison Ash steps aboard the *Persephone*, she knows her life will never be the same. (978-1-62639-938-9)

The Sniper's Kiss by Justine Saracen. The power of a kiss: it can swell your heart with splendor, declare abject submission, and sometimes blow your brains out. (978-1-62639-839-9)

Divided Nation, United Hearts by Yolanda Wallace. In a nation torn in two by a most uncivil war, can love conquer the divide? (978-1-62639-847-4)

Fury's Bridge by Brey Willows. What if your life depended on someone who didn't believe in your existence? (978-1-62639-841-2)

Lightning Strikes by Cass Sellars. When Parker Duncan and Sydney Hyatt's one-night stand turns to more, both women must fight demons past and present to cling to the relationship neither of them thought she wanted. (978-1-62639-956-3)

Love in Disaster by Charlotte Greene. A professor and a celebrity chef are drawn together by chance, but can their attraction survive a natural disaster? (978-1-62639-885-6)

Secret Hearts by Radclyffe. Can two women from different worlds find common ground while fighting their secret desires? (978-1-62639-932-7)

Sins of Our Fathers by A. Rose Mathieu. Solving gruesome murder cases is only one of Elizabeth Campbell's challenges; another is her growing attraction to the female detective who is hell-bent on keeping her client in prison. (978-1-62639-873-3)

Troop 18 by Jessica L. Webb. Charged with uncovering the destructive secret that a troop of RCMP cadets has been hiding, Andy must put aside her worries about Kate and uncover the conspiracy before it's too late. (978-1-62639-934-1)

Worthy of Trust and Confidence by Kara A. McLeod. Special Agent Ryan O'Connor is about to discover the hard way that when you can only handle one type of answer to a question, it really is better not to ask. (978-1-62639-889-4)

Amounting to Nothing by Karis Walsh. When mounted police officer Billie Mitchell steps in to save beautiful murder witness Merissa Karr, worlds collide on the rough city streets of Tacoma, Washington. (978-1-62639-728-6)

Crescent City Confidential by Aurora Rey. When romance and danger are in the air, writer Sam Torres learns the Big Easy is anything but. (978-1-62639-764-4)

Becoming You by Michelle Grubb. Airlie Porter has a secret. A deep, dark, destructive secret that threatens to engulf her if she can't find the courage to face who she really is and who she really wants to be with. (978-1-62639-811-5)

Love Down Under by MJ Williamz. Wylie loves Amarina, but if Amarina isn't out, can their relationship last? (978-1-62639-726-2)

Lightning Source UK Ltd.
Milton Keynes UK
UKOW01f2122280218
318660UK00001B/19/P